Fresh Air
The Bournemouth Writing Prize
2023 Shortlist

Fresher Publishing
Bournemouth University

Fresh Air
A Bournemouth Writing Prize anthology
First published 2023 by Fresher Publishing
Fresher Publishing
Bournemouth University
Weymouth House
Fern Barrow
Poole
Dorset BH12 5BB
www.fresherpublishing.co.uk
email publishing@bournemouth.ac.uk

Copyright © 2023 this collection: Fresher Publishing
Copyright © 2023 the stories: the authors

The authors have asserted their rights under the Copyright, Designs and Patents Act of 1988 to be identified as the authors of this work. This book may not be reproduced or transmitted in any form or by any means without the prior written consent of the publisher, except by a reviewer who wishes to quote brief passages in connection with a review written in a newspaper or magazine or broadcast on television, radio or on the internet.

Cover designed by: Chloe Moorehouse
Anthology designed by: Victoria Dence, Chloe Moorehouse, Leah Parker, Melissa Salcedo

Table of Contents

Foreword	XI
Acknowledgments	XIV
皮 Skin (Short Story Winner) *Kwan Ann Tan*	15
A Day at the Beach (Poetry Winner) *Emma Ormond*	25
Conversations with Foxes (Short Story Runner Up) *Sarah Humby*	29
Good People, Kind People (Short Story Runner Up) *Jay Mckenzie*	35
We Were Just Kids Ourselves (Highly Commended Short Story) *Rosie Chen*	43
Snowball Stand (Highly Commended Poem) *Matt Hohner*	51
The Thirteenth Floor (Highly Commended Short Story) *Richard Hooton*	53
the un. (Highly Commended Poem) *Jaz Slade*	65
Alice and the Whale (Highly Commended Short Story) *Ellie Taylor*	67

In the Slow Turning
Scott Elder   75

A letter to my grandson at the end of my life
Peter Endicott   77

Hypatia the First
Laura Gavin   87

Re-education Centre
Dean Gessie   99

Ms Fernandez
Ethel Hobby   103

To be on the Safe Side
Karen Hollands   107

Home thoughts at Red Rock, Nevada
Fin Keegan   117

Kleptophobia
Carmina Masoliver   119

Audition
Alex McDonald   123

Jam First
Ann Morgan   135

Glenferness Avenue
Thomas Riordan   145

Daddy Longlegs
  Mary Shovelin 147

Duffield
  Noel Taylor 157

Foreword

We are proud to introduce the 2023 Bournemouth Writing Prize Shortlist Anthology presented by Fresher Publishing. This carefully curated collection of short stories and poems features some of the most poignant, intriguing, and engrossing pieces from contemporary, up and coming writers and poets. From sandy beaches to suburban streets, contemporary literary fiction to speculative dystopia, every word, line, and sentence is a breath of fresh air through the pages.

The Bournemouth Writing Prize is an esteemed writing competition, opening the literary doors to writers and poets, both locally and internationally. Every year it showcases the short listed submissions and the winners's creations through the published anthologies. These anthologies celebrate the true values of writing. Giving a voice, and a blank page, to authors worldwide. It also plays an integral part in the MA Creative Writing and Publishing course at Bournemouth University, as it educates and encourages the students to develop their publishing talents through one of the units taught by the faculty of the Fresher Publishing team.

This year, the panel of judges consisted of professionals, all with renowned experiences in the literary world - poet Antony Dunn, writer and lecturer Bradford Gyori, commissioning editor Ansa Khan Khattak, author and narrative poet Tom Masters, and literary agent Julia Silk.

Antony Dunn, a four-time published poet, his most recent being 'Take This One to Bed', released in October 2016. He has won both an Eric Gregory Award and the Newgate Prize. When he isn't judging writing competitions, he's working hard as the Artistic Director of Bridlington

Poetry Festival.

Bradford Gyori currently leads the MA in Creative Writing and Publishing at Bournemouth University. His short fiction has been published in 'Café Irreal', 'No Parties Magazine', 'The Ghost Story', and 'Museums Journal'. His theatrical works have been presented by Steppenwolf, Phoenix Theatre, BEAF, and Poole Lighthouse. His recent digital productions include the location-aware drama Shelley's Heart and the immersive audio play, 'Mr. Illusion'.

Ansa Khan Khattak is a Commissioning Editor at Hutchinson Heinemann, where she works on both literary fiction and narrative non-fiction. Her authors include Lucia Berlin, Manohla Dargis, Wendy Erskine, Genki Kawamura, and Éric Vuillard.

Tom Masters is an author and lecturer currently teaching at Bournemouth University, where he teaches on the MA in Creative Writing & Publishing course. He holds a PhD in Creative & Critical Writing from the University of Winchester and has a special interest in narrative poetry.

Julia Silk has worked in publishing for over twenty years as an editor, bookseller, and, since 2016, as an agent. At Greyhound Literary she represents authors across the spectrum of commercial and literary fiction and narrative non-fiction and counts several short story writers among her clients, including Owen Booth, Amanda Mason, and Heidi James.

Our collection this year delves deep into themes of grief, family, and loneliness from a diverse range of authorial voices. Our short story winner, '皮 Skin' by Kwan Ann Tan, explores familial bonds across generational lines, and the poetry winner, 'A Day At The Beach' by Emma Ormond, offers a unique perspective on environmental anxiety and commercialisation. Alongside examinations of the mourning process through interactions with the animal kingdom, compelling speculative musings, and explorations of neighbourly relationships and ever changing family dynamics.

Finally, the editorial team would like to offer their personal congratulations to all of the shortlisted writers and, especially, to both of the winners and the highly commended and runner-up authors and poets. Further, to show our appreciation for the showcased talent, the editorial team would like to present their personal favourite entries which you can look out for alongside the judging panel's commentary throughout the anthology.

Acknowledgments

We would like to thank every writer who sent their work for Fresher Publishing's consideration. Each submission demonstrated immense imaginative vision and offered unique perspectives and it took considerable effort to reduce the entries into the presented shortlist.

As well, we would like to extend our gratitude to the current cohort of the Creating Writing and Publishing Master's Programme at Bournemouth University. The students took great care and pride in, first, working to select the longlist for the judging panel before producing the anthology presented before you today.

A further thanks and acknowledgment to all of the Fresher Publishing team for making the Bournemouth Writing Prize and anthology possible through their tireless work and devotion. Including, but not limited to, Editorial Director Tom Masters, Assistant Editorial Director Belinda Stuebinger, and Art Director Saeed Rashid.

In addition, we extend appreciation to this year's judging panel for their creation of the shortlist and winning entries. We would like to reiterate our thanks for their time and effort whilst working with Fresher Publishing. The standard of submissions for this year's competition ensured this was a difficult task but one the panel wholeheartedly embraced.

Last but not least, we would like to thank each and every reader for supporting each of the upcoming voices presented in this anthology. We hope you enjoy the work from this year's Bournemouth Writing Prize.

皮 Skin
Kwan Ann Tan

Kwan Ann Tan is a writer from Malaysia. Her work has previously been published in 'The Offing', 'Joyland Magazine', and 'Sine Theta Magazine', amongst others. You can find her at kwananntan.carrd.co or on Twitter: @KwanAnnTan

Judge's Comments
Funny, moving, engrossing, and with brilliant characterization and great writing – there were so many moments in this story that I loved. The ending is bold and strange, and shows exciting ambition. An extremely polished and accomplished piece of writing, in which every word earns its keep – I'd love to see more from this author.

皮 Skin
(Short Story Winner)

Every evening after dinner, when the dishes had been washed and put away, and the nighttime news on TV had died down, Jia Hui climbed the stairs to Po Po's bedroom to scratch her back.

Depending on the day of the week, sometimes there was something interesting to watch while she performed this task - a melodrama about crime and rich people on NTV7, a straight-to-TV-film that was set in the 70s, or a never-ending re-run of *Journey to the West* on 8TV, where Tang Sanzang stumbled again and again into traps set by beautiful women who were really just monsters, and monsters pretending to be beautiful women. Other times, Po Po just wanted to sit there and talk to Jia Hui, sometimes laying out her plans for the next day or gossiping excitedly about the neighbours. Occasionally, they would just sit in silence.

Jia Hui couldn't let herself become too absorbed in whatever they were watching or talking about at the time. Back scratching demanded a surprising amount of focus and care, especially since her grandmother's skin was now paper-thin and prone to injuries. Po Po hated using a backscratcher, no matter how many had been gifted to her over the years.

They are too harsh and rough, she complained. Like the claws of a monster scraping at your back.

Po Po would only let the people scratching her back use their fingers, the nails cut short. There didn't seem to be a certain method or way that Po Po preferred her back to be scratched, but everyone in the family had to try it at some point. Some met with instant approval, while others were given a little longer, like a trial period, then never allowed to scratch her back ever again.

Po Po started them young: as long as you had started school, you were old enough to scratch her back. At big family gatherings and holidays, she would call each grandchild to her in turn, asking them politely to scratch her back. Each grandchild would dutifully obey, abandoning whatever game they were playing to go over and give Po Po's back a half-hearted scratch. After Po Po was satisfied, she would give them a sweet and call the next grandchild to her. It was, as Po Po would tell Jia Hui, a good way of telling what kind of temperament the child would have later in life.

For example, Jia Hui's eldest cousin Calvin had scratched Po Po's back methodically, following each box of the checked shirt she had been wearing that day, then in patterns across, diagonally, and downwards. He was now a mathematician in the United States, where he worked on complex problems that Jia Hui could only dream of understanding. Another cousin, Helen, who was the same age as Jia Hui, had scratched Po Po's back at random, often getting distracted by everything around her, to the point that Po Po had to gently pull her attention back to the task at hand multiple times. Helen was now an aspiring fashion designer, had a parade of boyfriends at her heels, and still lived with her parents. One of Jia Hui's younger cousins, Zheng Wei, had gone a step further and argued with Po Po about why he shouldn't have to, laying out his arguments even as he begrudgingly scratched her back. He was now studying to become a criminal lawyer.

Jia Hui wondered if back then, just from the back scratching, Po Po was able to tell that only Jia Hui would be left behind to take care of her.

Jia Hui was a daughter of a daughter. Although on the

surface, her mother's family didn't seem to care much for those traditions, there was the lingering feeling that her time wasn't worth as much as the rest of the family's. Both her parents had died in a car crash when she was twelve, and Jia Hui had bounced around from aunt to uncle until she was old enough to go to university and live on her own. No one had been unkind, but she knew she was the family charity case and owed each of her relatives a debt for raising and taking care of her.

When Po Po had fallen and broken her arm, it became clear that Po Po couldn't live on her own anymore. But where could she go? Some of her own children were planning to emigrate, while others already had other parents to take care of. The logical solution, which even Jia Hui had convinced herself of now, was to find someone to move in and take care of Po Po.

And who better than Jia Hui? It wasn't as if she had a big career that she couldn't afford to lose - she had completed her degree in accounting overseas in the UK, thanks to the insurance money her parents had left behind, but she hadn't secured a job yet. None of the other grandchildren could be spared, not even Helen, who, truthfully, spent most of her days sleeping off the hangovers from the previous nights rather than actually designing any clothes. No, Jia Hui was the best choice. Besides, she was responsible, quiet, and clean. She was the perfect choice.

Jia Hui remembered when the family told her that she would have to return home. Po Po's eldest son, an uncle who worked at a bank and whose house Jia Hui disliked the most when she stayed there, had called her on the phone at four in the morning, completely disregarding the time zone difference (even though he had a son in the UK at that very moment).

Jia Hui knew that Po Po was in the hospital after her fall,

so her mind jumped to the worst. She quickly picked up the phone, stammering questions into the receiver.

'Ah-girl, calm down,' her uncle said, clearing his throat. 'Po Po is fine.'

Jia Hui nearly cried in relief. What else could he be calling about at this hour, though, if Po Po was fine? She waited again for him to speak, her heart calming down.

'We, I mean, all your aunties and uncles here think it's time for you to come home lah. Po Po misses you so much.'

Jia Hui frowned to herself. 'Da Jiu Jiu,' she said slowly. 'I can't leave now, I'm in the middle of my final exams. I called Po Po and told her that I would come home and visit her after that.'

Her uncle cleared his throat again, irritated that Jia Hui seemed to be missing the point.

'Not just visit. You should come home, live with Po Po and help take care of her. Do the right thing lah, huh?'

Jia Hui didn't say anything.

'It's the right thing to do,' her uncle repeated firmly. 'The right thing. We'll scrape together for your flight ticket and all, but it's expensive. We should book in advance, so we don't waste our money. You can slowly pay us back when you find a job. Text me the date that your exams finish.'

Even at a time like this, when he was asking her a favour, her uncle couldn't help but remind her how much of a burden she was on *all* of them, the collective we of the family. It was one of the reasons that she had avoided that family as much as possible.

She stayed quiet, which her uncle seemed to take as an agreement. What else was there left to say? Jia Hui knew that it was the right thing to do, and she did want to take care of her grandmother. She just resented being told it in this way, given an obligation, an order, when all he had to do was ask nicely.

'So… we settled this lah. No need to bring back anything for us, just come home as soon as possible. Thanks.' He hung up.

Two weeks later, Jia Hui had stuffed as much of her life as she could in the two suitcases she owned, said goodbye to a handful of friends, and landed at KLIA, where no one was there to meet her. After making the two hour, three-train, and one bus journey by LRT from the airport, she finally arrived at Po Po's house. This was the beginning of the rest of her life.

The thing was, Jia Hui truly loved Po Po. Sometimes, when the relatives she was staying with at the time went on vacation, they left her at Po Po's place, where they would take trips to the seaside and drag the sand for little clams. Po Po was the only one who didn't get irritated when Jia Hui had another nightmare about her parents' funeral, her dreams filled with their bodies lying still like wax figures in a child's fevered hallucination of the car crash that had taken their lives. In those dreams, Jia Hui tried to reach into the fire and drag them out, but they were so heavy, waterlogged with flames. Po Po would sit up with her, soothing and scratching gentle circles on Jia Hui's back until she fell asleep.

When Jia Hui scratched Po Po's back, it was an act of love.

That night, like every night before and every night that was to come, Jia Hui scratched Po Po's back carefully, occasionally lingering at a spot when directed to and paying special attention to avoid areas that were sore or irritated. She knew Po Po's back better than her own, which she only caught in half-glimpses in the mirror, craning her neck until it hurt.

The skin on Po Po's back was wrinkled and sagging,

but it stretched slightly as she hunched over. In the half-light from her bedside lamp, it looked to Jia Hui as if the ridged, slightly raised bones of her spine was the seam of an eyelid, ready to open at any time. It struck Jia Hui that she had seen something similar before in a thousand-year-old manuscript at a museum exhibition.

It was the margins of the manuscript that first caught Jia Hui's attention. The text was too fine and spiky for her to read, but all around the neat block of script were eyes of different sizes and shapes. She had idly noticed annotations and notes around most of the other manuscripts, but this one did not have any words in the margin, only eyes studded unevenly around the text like dark, inky lesions. At the beginning of the exhibition, she remembered reading that the manuscripts were usually made of parchment, which in turn was made from animal skins scrubbed so thin that you could shine a light through them. The piece of skin they had on display was stretched painfully taut and reminded her of the *wayang kulit* from home, shadow puppets playing against the flickering light. Here, no matter how much Jia Hui squinted at the book, she could not make out any trace of blue-green veins, or even the faint blush of rosy skin. Yet, the dried skin reminded her of the papery translucence of a peeling sunburn when a particularly satisfying flap of dead skin had been lifted from the reddened new skin, or the slightly yellowed skin that flaked off her toes when she contracted foot fungus in secondary school from wearing someone else's shoes. In the manuscript she was currently looking at, the eyes bulged out ever-so-slightly, the ink and parchment swollen after so many years. Each eye stared back blankly.

As Jia Hui's gaze shifted from one eye to the next, and she felt herself going into a trance, the eyes fading in and out of her periphery as she traced her own eyes around them. If she let her eyes drift out of focus, the eyes on the book seemed as if they were all looking back at her, the book apprehending her from its glass cage. The deep black letters with their sharp horns and boxy edges looked far too close to the drawn eyes, making her flinch slightly as she imagined the tail of a pointed g poking into the soft flesh of the drawn eyes. Po Po's skin turned into a page, filled with spiky writing and with eyelids that peeled themselves back from the smooth skin to turn into real eyes, darting to look around in the sharp, beady way that Po Po's own eyes moved.

Jia Hui didn't stop scratching, so she instead traced patterns around the eyes, not daring to get too close. The moving letters and eyes made it difficult. If she wasn't afraid of poking her finger on the sharp flick of a long-stemmed letter, then she was terrified of accidentally poking one of the eyes and causing any pain to Po Po.

Her fingers got closer and closer to Po Po's spine as the eyes opened and closed in a pattern that seemed completely random. The bones of the spine were the guiding line for her fingers. Jia Hui scratched carefully, up, then down, until she felt a shift.

It was a slow awakening, a rumbling that made tiny tremors up and along the curved bones. Jia Hui's scratching slowed as she watched the transformation, and then she stopped altogether.

Po Po's spine split open to reveal a watery, red-veined eye that seemed confused at its sideways orientation, like a sleeper wondering where they were. Jia Hui reared back, nearly falling off the plastic stool she sat on. The eye looked directly at Jia Hui, and then sealed itself back up, smoothing out into the familiar lines and folds of Po Po's back.

'Jia Hui?' She saw Po Po's concerned face in the round

mirror to the side. 'Are you okay?'

When Jia Hui didn't answer, Po Po turned to look back. The lights flickered for a moment - not uncommon for the old house - but Jia Hui only saw Po Po's luminous eyes in the dark, staring blankly at her.

A Day at the Beach
Emma Ormond

Emma Ormond is a poet from Cambridge, England. She holds a PhD in Insect Ecology and references to plants, invertebrates, and animals feature heavily in her work. Her poems have appeared in three anthologies and she was a runner up in the inaugural Fenland Poet Laureate (2013) and Ealing Autumn Festival Poetry Competition (2014), most recently her poem 'Heritage' received a special mention in the 2021 Bournemouth Writing Prize.

Judge's Comments
I've never before judged a poetry competition in which the first poem I read went on to be the winner. But this is the one. 'A Day at the Beach' struck me immediately with its confidence, its sure-footedness with line breaks and stanza breaks, faults in which helped to keep some other promising poems off the top spot.

It's a poem that gives itself over to the reader gradually, disturbingly. It feels planned, paced, and purposeful. It suggests itself into the conversation about the climate crisis at a slant angle – bordering on the fantastical but, at the same time, a horrifyingly believable glimpse into the near future. It's a wry and measured take on the commercialization of our collective demise, the consumers of rare experiences helpless in the confluence of their own desire and the inexorable machinery of money.

The disruption to the form of the poem as it nears its conclusion feels compelling rather than accidental, the multiple-choice list of feedback options preventing negative feedback, and the final, single-line stanza packs a breath-taking wallop in its brevity.

I'm delighted to have read 'A Day at the Beach' and I'm very pleased indeed to award it first prize for a poem in the Bournemouth Writing Prize 2023.

A Day at the Beach
(Poetry Winner)

I spot her from the deck, mid-mimosa sip
instinctively check her wrist, *day-pass kid*,
best-dressed, nauseated on excitement,
so many never see the ocean.

She trips, her first experience of sand,
how softly it shifts beneath her feet,
how it still swipes the air from her lungs,
abrades her palms the same as concrete.

Her family settle down, cheap beach kit
they'll probably only use it once,
someone told me the average wait time
7 years a ticket if you register at conception.

She can't swim, paddles instead
no deeper than her ankles: mother calls,
entranced she collects small pebbles,
decorates a sandcastle, buries her feet.

By lunchtime their slot is expiring,
packed-up back up to the gates,
security check failed: she gives up her pebble,
souvenirs are not included in the price of this day-pass.

They take the exit survey: names? ages?
How much do you agree with the following statements?

This beach experience is:

Forward-Thinking
Familiar
New and Different
Good Value for Money
Exciting
For People Like Me

While the turnstiles roll people in and out like the tide.

Conversations with Foxes
Sarah Humby

Sarah Humby is quite an old woman now, but a new writer. A visual artist by trade, writing is a habit she came to late in life, during the wee small hours of unsleep, to distract from insomnia and brain fog. She likes to focus on the minutiae of daily living, the everyday things we do to 'get by' that make up a lifetime. You will find her on the coast staring out to sea, clutching a pencil, with a small dog at her feet.

Judge's Comments
A short powerful story about loss. I loved the strangeness of the fox's appearance and the way the narrator's grief is skilfully woven-in and gradually revealed. I loved the spareness and restraint of the writing, in contrast to the depth of emotion – a great example of less being more.

Conversations with Foxes

There was a fox in the bedroom again, staring at its own reflection in the mirrored door of the wardrobe.

It was sitting on the pink rag rug I'd made for Elspeth and, from there, he watched me enter the room. In the time it took me to make the split-second decision not to run, and instead to remain still, I could tell that this was also a decision he was weighing up. He, too, did not bolt.

'What are you doing here?' I asked. I'm not sure if I said it out loud but if I did, it was under my breath.

I gently stepped forward and eased myself down to a kneeling position at the foot of Elspeth's bed and rested my head on the soft toys she'd kept there. The fox sat motionless, but all the while our eyes remained locked in the reflected glass.

'What are you doing here?' I asked again.

He didn't reply. His snout was long and bony, and his eyes glistened like quicksilver. The thick russet fur on his tail was tinted burnt sienna with a tip of pure white. There was white hair, too, on the soft inner part of his ears and peppered across his forehead and eyes. He was not a young fox. I wanted him to tell me that I would be alright. That grief wouldn't kill me. I wanted him to tell me that Elspeth wasn't really gone.

The golden light of the early autumn evening was beginning to fade, and a soothing breeze through the net curtains brushed my face with the air of a cooling day. The streetlights would click on eventually, but for now, the remnants of low sunlight played across the wall, illuminating the space where the fox still sat.

I reached out, picked up a stray toy from the floor, and studied it for a while. The fox made no move to leave but observed me silently. The toy, a tiny wooden doll small enough to fit in the palm of my hand, was staring at me, too. But not with pity or recrimination, nor even with kindness. Just a doll waiting to be held. My father, a joiner, had made it for me many years ago when I was just a child myself. It wore a fading, painted smile, and clothes fashioned by Elspeth to replace the ones she'd originally worn. She had written her name across the forearm of the doll in faint, staggered writing. She was learning so much, so quickly, and craved knowledge.

'What's the smallest thing in the world, Mummy?'
'How do you know when it's going to rain?'
'How does the moon stay up?'
'Why are foxes' tail tips white?'

That last, about foxes' tails, was in the spring, when we watched them in the street playing in the snow after a freakishly late, unseasonably cold snap. We were in her room, *this* room, and she was transfixed. She'd been ill for some time, and we were nearing the end, stepping tenderly through each new day, trying to avoid thinking about the future. She was connected to an oxygen pump by a long thin thread of plastic tubing, like an umbilical cord, which administered a steady stream of air to her failing lungs. It sat in the corner of the room humming constantly and made a noise like a distant lawnmower, or someone digging softly into gravel.

I don't know why some foxes' tails are white at the tip, so I told her something about how it was so that other foxes could see them in the dark. I knew that wasn't right, but I needed to tell her something. I needed her to think I had at least some answers, and some lies *are* that easy to tell. Others, of course, are not. She didn't really know how ill she was.

When she asked if she was going to get better, I said,

'Yes, of course you will, my darling.'

I held the lie within me like grit in my sock, or a hair in my eye. It felt small and insubstantial, but ever present. A little dagger to punctuate the overwhelming feelings of suffocation and impending grief. The digging in of that lie, repetitive and painful, helped to keep me breathing. Like someone poking me in the chest, constantly urging me onward, to keep me stepping forward. To contemplate the days to come, without her, whilst her father sat crumpled in a ragged heap somewhere a million miles away, in some other corner of the house.

The fox stirred and turned his wise old head toward me, drawing my attention away from the wooden doll. I wanted him to tell me that she'd never doubted me, and that she'd trusted me.

The room was dark now, the air beginning to chill. I moved from my position on the floor, hauled myself onto the bed, and lay there heavily while the fox sat at its ease, as though in meditation. Elspeth would have had some questions about this, I thought. It was the first time I'd considered her in the past tense without the usual attendant smothering waves of deep, deep self-indulgent sorrow. Always, I seemed to be drowning, but never was I allowed to drown. There was silence in her room as the streetlights flickered on. The night came creeping in, to haunt me in that room.

The fox slipped away as I half slept, fitfully at the end of the child's bed. The doll clutched hotly in my hand, the silken cover bunched and damp with tears under my head. I sensed his movement as he slinked past sometime in the early morning, and I thought I caught the white tip of his tail from the corner of my half-closed eyes as he slipped off down the dimly lit hallway.

In the morning, from the kitchen, I saw him again and

startled him in the garden as I opened the back door to let the fresh air in. He stared at me, and I stared back. After a short moment, his attention diverted, he was gone. I'd like to think that he'd say everything was going to be alright. Some lies are that easy to tell.

Good People, Kind People
Jay Mckenzie

Jay McKenzie's short stories, flash, and micros have been published online at 'Cafe Lit Magazine', 'Sadie Tells Stories', 'Save As' and 'Off Topic', and in print in 'Mr Rosewood', 'Fabula Nivalis', 'Leicester Writes', 'The Gift' and 'Crimson', 'Unleash Lit Magazine', and 'Cerasus Magazine'. She is a two time winner of Furious Fiction and winner of the 2022 Exeter Story Prize. Her debut novel will be published in 2023 with Australian indie press Serenade Publishing.

Judge's Comments
A brilliantly realistic story about people and their limitations – the author explores the gulf between how we like to think of ourselves and who we actually are incredibly well. Great descriptive writing, which made it a beautifully visual story. The final line lands incredibly powerfully.

Good People, Kind People

'But we are good people, kind people.' Antonia smiles. 'And we brought you this welcome gift. It's a flowering cactus, grown by Elspeth at number eight.'

The man stares at the plant uncomprehendingly. His eyes look as though they only work part-time and spend the rest of their hours tucked cosily in the crumpled blankets of the crow's feet folds on his fleshy face.

'I...no...Ingliss,' he stammers.

That Antonia's pithy welcome speech has fallen on deaf ears makes me laugh, but the icy glare she throws my way frightens the giggle into a cough. She peers beyond the man down the dark hallway of number nine.

'Is. There. Anyone. Else. Here? Hmm? That. Speaks. English?' The volume has risen, the pace slowed to a near standstill. *Brilliant Antonia,* I think. *That'll help.*

We stand awkwardly. Apart from the man at number nine and Antonia, there's Antonia's husband Harry, Liz and Beth from number five, and me here. We're a neatly pressed, fragrant army, all Ralph Lauren and suburban smug. For a moment, I see us from the man's perspective and hate us, just a little.

'Well,' says Antonia in a clipped alto. 'We'll see you around.' She pushes the plant pot into the old man's hands, turns and stalks through us up the path. We follow, of course. I wave at the man as he watches us retreat. He nods, frowns again, and closes the door.

We convene at Antonia's for a glass of wine under the premise that 'it's nearly the weekend'.

'Well,' says Antonia, cool Chablis poured into their Gabriel-Glas ware. 'What do you make of the old man?'

Liz takes a sip of her wine. 'It's hard to tell, isn't it? With the,' she pauses, 'language barrier and all.'

We nod our agreement.

'Still. He could have smiled at least. When he saw that we were bringing him a plant.'

'You know,' says Harry, 'we probably caught him in the middle of unpacking.'

Murmurs of assent.

'Unpacking's a bore,' says Beth. 'I still haven't unpacked my hand luggage from Dubai!'

We titter. *Oh, Beth! Aren't you terrible?*

Nibbling the canapés that Antonia 'had lying in the fridge' we chat about Beth and Liz's trip, the extension Elspeth is building and Antonia's home office renovations. What we're thinking about though is how that little old man can afford to rent the Delaney's place.

'Maybe he's a professor of some sort,' my husband Jack speculates. 'They're always kind of crumpled.'

'Who doesn't speak English?'

'Perhaps he's got a translator. Ooh, maybe he's an expert at something niche!'

'Maybe.'

I'm unlocking my car when a taxi pulls up outside number nine. A woman bundled in bulky layers steps out of the cab holding a baby. Two children climb out of the other side, eyes wide. The woman fires some rapid instructions in a language I don't recognise at the children who scoot around the car to her side.

They retrieve bags from the boot: a large holdall, two canvas shopping bags and four, thin plastic ones. As the laden party waddle up the path to number nine, I take a quick snap on my iPhone and send it to Antonia.

'Thank you for seeing us, Neil.'

Antonia and I are in one of the glass-fronted offices of Hawthorns Suburban Lettings agency sipping cool iced tea. I was the only other resident working from home today, and Antonia can be hard to say no to.

'It's not that we're being judgemental, Neil. It's just that the Delaney's usually rent to professional families, and well, the new occupants don't seem like the previous residents.'

'Ah,' says Neil, running a finger under the collar of his shirt. 'Yes, well, this is a slightly different... situation.'

'Oh?' Antonia puts her glass on the table, beads of condensation dripping like glimmering diamonds.

Neil shifts in his seat. 'I'm afraid it's not appropriate to disclose further details.'

'Of course.' Antonia smiles. 'But we are good people. Kind people. We can help the family to assimilate so much better if we know about them. Plus, it's our duty to Meg and Brian Delaney to ensure that their home is being looked after properly.'

'Quite.'

Antonia keeps her eyes on Neil, a half-smile and slow blink the only movement. I glance at the clock and wait.

'The Delaney's offered to house a refugee family.'

Six seconds before Neil cracked! I grin.

'I see.'

'Their previous tenants weren't renewing, and Meg's got some Ukrainian heritage. She wanted to help out.'

Antonia picks up her drink, takes a slow sip. 'How very selfless of them.'

She waits until we're outside. 'I've got an idea.'

Oksana ushers the family into Antonia's formal lounge. She nods politely at the assembled as the new residents of the Delaney's house shuffle across the polished oak floor. We watch, as though they are a novelty after-dinner cabaret act. The old man who answered the door that day stands close to Oksana, the other woman has the baby strapped to her front in a simple scarf, favoured by the boho mums who use cloth nappy laundry services. The two children hover at her heels.

'Welcome!' says Antonia loudly. 'Oksana, can you tell them we say welcome.'

Oksana addresses the old man, her mouth barely moving as she flings out a rapid string of words that sounds longer than a straightforward welcome. I wonder how much Antonia and Harry are paying her for the night. The man nods politely when she finishes but doesn't respond.

Antonia's voice sounds disturbingly bright. 'It's lovely to have them here. We'd love to learn all about them. Wouldn't we, everyone?'

We all nod. There are twelve of us, discounting Oksana and the family. It's not easy to distinguish which of us are here to welcome them and which are afraid to say no to Antonia. Grayson Arnold is clearly only here for the wine, which he's sinking with gleeful abandon.

'Could you ask them to tell us all about themselves?'

There's a volley of words between Oksana and the man, accompanied by shrugs and frowns. The woman with the baby glances around the room at the large-scale pieces of contemporary art, including an original Adelaide Damoah, which Harry likes to say they got 'for a steal'.

'His name is Fedir Koval. He did maintenance in a steel plant. This is his daughter-in-law, Inna and his grandchildren.'

Interesting, we murmur. *Lovely.*

'And the son,' says Naomi from twelve. *The* son, not *his* son, or *her* husband or *their* father: *the* son. 'Is he involved in the troubles?'

Oksana's face reddens. She doesn't even translate for Fedir. 'Yes. His son is fighting for his country.'

We mill around nibbling blinis and sipping Pimms. Inna screws up her face as she takes a drink from a fruit-laden glass and tucks it behind a vase. The little boy pokes a mini cheesecake but doesn't eat it. Everyone takes it in turns to step up to Oksana and ask the family a well-considered question. I'm wracking my brain for something pertinent, yet sensitive to say when Oksana announces that the family want to go to bed. She avoids the word 'home'.

'Of course, of course,' flaps Antonia. 'Silly me. They're probably still jetlagged.'

'Oh, I got terrible jetlag coming back from New Zealand,' says Elspeth. We grimace in sympathy.

'Before they go Oksana, could you just translate this for me please?' Oksana stifles a yawn, but nods. 'As the Mad Hatter says, "we're all mad here".' We laugh politely. 'But we are good people. Kind people. And we want them to feel like they're one of us.'

I wince at the pomposity of the *us*, while Oksana translates. When she finishes, Fedir looks doubtful.

'I had the Jubilee Street Party flyer translated into Ukrainian. I'll drop it in today.'

We're drinking French Earl Grey while going over the decorations for the celebration.

'Did it specify about moving the cars?' asks Liz. 'Because - and you know I *love* the Korvarals dearly - but that Cortina is an eyesore, and we've got *The Herald* coming.'

'Of course!' Antonia drums her fingers on the mood board. 'And I've even had extra bunting made for them, so they don't need to worry about it.'

How kind, I think. *They've nothing more pressing than bunting on their minds at the moment.*

Inna has been looking red-eyed the last few times I've seen her, when she takes the three children for walks to the park. I wave, but the most I've got from her is a nod. Fedir hasn't left the house. People come and go though, sometimes with bags, other times with clipboards. I hope they're okay.

Antonia's fists are jammed into her hips. I follow her gaze, fixed on the rusty gold Cortina outside number nine.

'They didn't get the message, huh?'

'Oh, they got the message all right!' She digs her phone out of her pocket and hits the keypad, bringing the phone to her ear. 'I used Google translate *and* got Oksana to check it over. Hello?' She ends the call. 'Bloody voicemail. I've been calling Oksana all morning!'

The street flutters with red, white and blue bunting. Trestle tables line the road, Union flag tablecloths held down by cake stands and juice pitchers. The Korval's car stands alone, everyone else having moved theirs last night.

'Good job there's all that space by the boatsheds,' said Jack last night, returning for the Merc after parking his BMW.

'Come with me,' commands Antonia. 'I'll use semaphore if I have to.'

She tears across the road and up the pathway of number nine. I notice how weedy the garden has grown in the weeks since the Korval's moved in. *Last thing on their minds,* I think.

I follow Antonia, who's rapping on the door with her bony white knuckles. The door opens a crack, Inna's face framed by long, limp hair.

'Hello, Inna.' Antonia is smiling, but her words are clipped. 'The car. The car needs to be moved.' She points at the car, mimes driving, then points to the end of the road. 'I will move it, if you give me the keys. The. Keys.'

Inna opens the door a little and pokes her face out, frowning. Down the middle of her head, a crease dissects the two sides, a faultline on her face. Her eyes look scratched and raw.

'No Inglis,' she says. 'No Inglis.'

'You don't need English to know that I want you to move

the car.' Antonia digs the translated flyer out of her pocket and waves it at Inna.

'Antonia...' I put my hand on her arm, but she flicks me away like an annoying fly.

'I got this translated for you. See, here. Move the car. No cars on the street.'

'Antonia!' Sharper this time. Inna's eyes are brimming.

'Ellen, we are good people. Kind people. I've gone out of my way to make these people feel welcome.' She shakes her head at Inna. 'But this Jubilee party has been months in the planning. Special permits, entertainment licences, alcohol licences, and *translation* services that I hadn't budgeted for.'

'Antonia, stop.'

The door to number nine swings fully open. A woman I've never seen before speaks to Inna in a hushed voice. Inna wails, the woman wrapping her into an embrace. She glares at us over Inna's heaving shoulder.

'What do you want?' She has a slight accent overlaying the educated English.

'Ah!' Antonia, either failing to notice or choosing to ignore the woman's obvious hostility, is clearly delighted to have a translation service at her fingertips. 'We need her to move the car so we can have our street party.'

'Street party?' The woman practically spits. 'Street party? This woman's husband is missing.' She pushes Inna into the house. 'Fuck your street party and fuck you!'

The door slams in our faces. Antonia turns to me, eyes wide, brimming with tears. 'But we are good people. Kind people.'

We Were Just Kids Ourselves
Rosie Chen

Rosie Chen is based in London, where she manages a recording studio. Her short stories have appeared in 'The Mays Anthology' and Desperate Literature's 'Eleven Stories' collection. She is currently working on her first novel, 'Jimmy the Food Thief', which was a finalist in Hachette UK's Mo Siewcharran Prize 2021. It was also longlisted for the Lucy Cavendish College Fiction Prize 2022.

Judge's Comments
Written in an immediately arresting tone, there's a brilliant dark humour to this story of what it feels like to step into someone else's life. The second person can be hard to pull off but is handled really well here, giving a strong sense of immediacy to the story; great upmarket commercial writing.

We Were Just Kids Ourselves

After his daughter, and his ex-wife, you are the most important woman in this man's life. His ex-wife is important to him, not because he still loves her - although you assume he still does - but because she is and will always be the woman who gave him a family. The labour was difficult, and they were happy together for a long time. You do not have a family of your own, so, of course you do not understand what this means. When you ask him to tell you about his favourite birthdays, he hesitates, and her calls take precedence over yours. She could be calling about Hannah. You are only ever calling for yourself.

To Hannah you are the white woman who pushed her mother out of the lock screen on his phone. To her credit, this is not untrue; the picture that flashes up on his screen used to have all three of them in it. It was a picture taken at his sister's wedding, where Hannah was a bridesmaid. The bride and groom stood in the middle, with their families on either side. You do not mind particularly that he has a past - everyone has a past - but you got sick of seeing his ex-wife's face whenever you checked his phone for the time. Now, out of respect for your existence, his background is a dutiful father-daughter-only photo: he's pink as a rose and there's sun in their eyes. His ex-wife is behind the camera, probably, adjusting the straps of her swimming costume as the two people who love her most in the world assemble to take the picture.

You can remember the first picture ever taken with you in it: a selfie from the day that Hannah was forced to accompany you and him to the travelling fair. They used to go together, as a family, when Hannah was little, and although you are all too big for the rides now, he insisted on taking you both there. He made you and Hannah sit next to each other on the Ferris wheel. She wrinkled her nose, like you were a bad smell, and pulled herself so close to the edge of the carriage that your legs were not touching at all. What did people think, when they saw you and her and him, silently biting into candy apples and queuing up for tokens? You look at the photo, and it gives you heartburn. She looks like a supermodel, a pop star; she's only fifteen, but she looks older than that. You and he look like you have won a competition to be there.

His ex-wife, who is Asian, is a much better person than you are. She wears beige shift dresses, chews with her mouth open, she cares about animals, she is five years older than him, and she makes her own cleaning products out of vinegar and baking soda. Although she has lived in this country for the past twenty-three years, she does not speak English very well. All her friends are Asian. Several of them have white husbands. She has kept his bed warm for nearly half your life, and during that time she made him believe in something greater than himself. He has eaten scorpions because of her. He has climbed volcanoes. There are sauces in the cupboard, and you don't know what they're for. He still wears slippers all the time, because she did, and he says that she's told Hannah to be nice.

Despite her mother's instructions, Hannah continues to torture you. It is only women, in your experience, who know exactly where to twist the knife. She tries on your clothes, and they drown her. She closes her door and shrieks at her friends down the phone. She leaves dimples in your expensive moisturiser. She wants to know why all the authors on your bookshelf are white. She thinks that she's a renegade because she once bleached the ends of her hair, and she comes home from parties smelling of smoke - but she is nothing like you used to be at her age, and when the ends of her hair came out orange instead of blonde, she cried for a whole day. Sometimes it feels less like you are her father's new girlfriend and more like you are her ugly stepsister. You find the little scraps of poetry that she writes in her neat handwriting, and you wonder whether she is doing this on purpose or if it's all in your head. You hear her practising the violin, and she's moderately talented.

Being divorced from a woman who is Asian is different from being divorced from a woman who is not. For example, he is obliged to pretend that they are still married for the benefit of his in-laws. Once a month, he returns to the family home, to which you are granted access only on special occasions. Where they put up their old holiday pictures in the living room, and they video call his ex-wife's wrinkled parents for an hour. He parks his silver Ford Mondeo in the driveway like he always has. You think, surely not, but you watch from your car on the other side of the road, and it's true. They take turns holding the phone. They drink boiled water and eat peanuts. They will continue this pretence for as long as it takes for his ex-wife's parents to die because they don't believe in divorce in their culture, apparently.

Would it be better if you were Asian, too? You look in the bathroom mirror and peel your eyes back into slits - although you would never do this in company and would not condone it if you saw it, say, in passing. You even go as far as miming the words *okay meester* and *ling long*, *ching chong*, jerking your head like the woman who serves you at the Chinese takeaway - not because you are racist, no, but because it feels really good to do something that you're not supposed to, if only for a moment, on your own. You press your hands together and bow until you can no longer see your reflection. You giggle behind cupped fingers. You decide that, overall, it's a good thing you're not Asian. If you were Asian, Hannah might think that her father had a fetish, and she would probably turn out to be right.

Hannah lives with her mother, but she spends every other weekend with you and him; she has her own room in his house, which is more than you can say. When Hannah is not there, you sneak into her room and finger the drapes that she chose. She does not keep real clothes there, only socks and a selection of large t-shirts. There are prints taped to the wall above her bed, and an anatomical line drawing of a heart, and a naked picture of John Lennon and Yoko Ono - who has an enormous bush, by the way, her pubes are thick and wiry. You have seen pictures of him and her as a young couple, and sometimes you feel you know exactly what it was like back then, as you picture his wet mouth pressed against Yoko Ono's enormous breasts.

Hannah's fortnightly visits are characterised by sit-down dinners and organised physical activities: axe-throwing, ping pong, crazy golf. Most of the other participants are there on dates, but on Fridays there are office workers of a similar demographic out for an enforced social. He takes you and her bouldering one time, and the sight of Hannah in her toffee-coloured gym leggings makes you want to throw away all the fat and carbs from your fridge. He wants her to race him to the top of the wall, but she pulls a face like he's asked her to kiss him on the mouth. You get the sense that she does not like her father very much, but at least she likes him more than you.

Afterwards, there is space for conversation. You are delighted to discover that Hannah likes music. She helps you unpack the groceries that you picked up on the way home from the ice rink, bowling alley, trampoline park, and you take the opportunity to play her some of the artists you think she will like - Joni Mitchell, Bob Dylan, The Smiths. You try to show off about who you saw live as a teenager, and your cheeks twitch. But she only scowls at you. You leave your songs on in the kitchen as you make white food for dinner, and while you are bent over the oven to check on the progress of the casserole, she Shazams her favourites under the table.

On Sunday night, Hannah goes home. You wait a while, and then you ask him the questions that you were too scared to ask her. Did Hannah have any pets growing up? Would Hannah like to watch *Sliding Doors* with us? You lie beside him and look his daughter up online, like she's a celebrity or something. You can't find her on Facebook. He tells you that she has some kind of joke username - but you find her on Instagram; three Asian characters are printed in her bio, beside a black and white profile picture that doesn't show her face. You paste the characters into Google, and it translates to something pornographic - 'Moonlight Fantasy' or similar - and he tells you that's the name her mother gave her. Almost on a daily basis, you resist the urge to remind Hannah that she is just as white as she is Asian. But you don't get to tell her how to belong in either place, nor would you want to, and so you judge her silently while her father grunts himself to sleep beside you.

There had been a guy before this one, who was nice while it lasted. You had talked loosely about children. You had talked about children with boyfriends before him - in dopey voices, fingers interlaced - but with this one, at your age, it was no longer roleplay. Anyway, the whole thing with that guy ran its course - you parted ways amicably, still talk occasionally - and you realised that this was how it would end all along, that it was never going to happen for you. More than anything, you are furious that it is not yet too late for him to become a father. You will never forgive him for what he has not yet done. You wait for the news, splashed out on your computer screen in blue and gold: all your boyfriends, past and present, now have children that are not yours.

You are angry that you care, it's unoriginal. You spy the books on Hannah's shelf about feminism, and you hope that caring makes her angry too. One day you would like to show her things, but when you try to engage her in conversation, she frowns at you and uses words you don't understand. Although you don't really disagree with her, she makes you feel like you do. Her father seems to think that you do, anyway; he holds his arms aloft and tells you and her, unasked, that he is not getting involved. You are not sure about the future with him, but right now you want to marry him, because with those hands in the air he might have fixed everything. You glance at Hannah in a gesture of solidarity - 'Men, ey?' - but in the time that it has taken for him to interrupt she has already returned to her phone.

Your friends tell you sagely that this is the hardest part. If you and he make it far enough, she will grow up and you will only see her on public holidays and in times of crisis, and by then it will be much easier. Even further, and you might even be a grandmother - although her generation, maybe they're not into that. You substitute an elderly version of yourself into the old material anyway, the hazy montage of sticky fingers and days at the beach. Everyone knows that being a grandparent's the best bit. Now you will cradle her babies in your arms and babysit on weekends while the world around you burns to cinders, probably.

If you and he make it further still, she will be there after you die. You hold the thought to your chest like a balm. When you're old, and especially when you're dead, you will be forgiven for most things. Everyone's nice to dead people. You turn the image over in your head: a suburban cemetery, the sinking sky. Hannah is older than you are now, laying genetically modified flowers at your grave as your body begins to rot, and it was not your fault that you were white, and the other half of her was not.

The Snowball Stand
Matt Hohner

Matt Hohner has won or placed in numerous national and international poetry competitions, including wins in the Doolin International Poetry Prize in Ireland, the 'Oberon Magazine' Poetry Prize, and the Maryland Writers' Association Prize. His publications include 'Rattle: Poets Respond', 'Sky Island Journal', 'The Cardiff Review', 'The Storms Journal', 'New Contrast, Live Canon', and 'Prairie Schooner'. An editor with 'Loch Raven Review', Hohner's first collection 'Thresholds and Other Poems' (Apprentice House) was published in 2018.

Judge's Comments
I enjoyed meandering along with this poem, really unsure where it was taking me. When it resolves, it does so mysteriously, but there's a sense of dislocation, or homesickness, that gives the poem an exquisitely painful exit-wound.

The Snowball Stand

We ordered from the cracked concrete alley
over the chain-link fence at the oak-shaded
end of a backyard behind Hardwick Road.
Flavoured, frozen candy water cost 75 cents, a
buck for a large, another quarter for marshmallow
sauce, if we wanted the extra tooth rot. Yellow
jackets drawn by the syrup buzzed the stand,
harassed the kids who ran it like they owned
the place. The snowball machine resembled
a meat grinder: crude weapon of shiny steel,
its flat-ended lever muscling whole icebergs
through what sounded like war. The aftermath
on the other side was obliteration, destruction,
drifts of jagged, hard granules like nor'easter
sleet. They hand-formed a mini Mount St. Helens
above the rim of the Styrofoam cup, their palms
bright red from sculpting winter all day, squirted
four or five vivid jets of high-fructose concentrate
into the middle, a little frozen volcano of frosty
relief from the sweltering caldera of Mid-Atlantic
summers. A long-handled white plastic spoon
brought it to the lips. It was gone before we
got home a block-and-a-half away. Hawaiian ice
is laid-back and feathery, like rainbow-striped
dreams floating in a cone-shaped cup. Shaved
ice, too, gives itself softly, easily to the hot mouth.
But Baltimore snowballs, winter storms in a cup,
fight back, shred the over-eager mouth, paralyse
with brain-freeze, require effort and guts and pain
like it does to live here. Everything here is a fight.
Even the sweet things. Especially the sweet things.

The Thirteenth Floor
Richard Hooton

Born and brought up in Mansfield, Nottinghamshire, Richard Hooton studied English Literature at the University of Wolverhampton before becoming a journalist and communications officer. He has had numerous short stories published and has won or been listed in various competitions. Richard lives in Mossley, near Manchester.

Judge's Comments
Dark and slightly chilling, the world of this story leapt off the page. I was really gripped – great storytelling and the voice was strong and well-judged. A brilliant ending.

The Thirteenth Floor

The lift feels as suffocating as being the smallest piece inside a Russian doll. Something distracts Mikhail though. A black scrawl on burnished chrome; the large letters dripping like blood from a wound. The teenager's hollow-cheeked face reflects back at him, raised eyebrows disappearing under an unruly mop of curly hair, petrol-blue eyes wide. He doesn't know if the sentence is poetry or philosophy or protest. It seems to be a call to arms.

The unexamined life is not worth living

Mikhail has never seen the sky, a sunset or snowfall. Nor a field or forest, mountain or lake. He's never savoured a breeze cooling his face or marvelled at a rainbow's magic. He's travelled every inch of The Block that he's allowed access to. Multiple times. With no windows or doors to the outside, there's nothing left to discover. The Block is his whole existence, one carefully mapped out for him. Mikhail looks at the buttons: one to thirteen. Every now and then his finger hovers over the higher number, but he knows it's forbidden to even think about going there. He jabs button one. Waits for the stomach-sinking descent.

The lift stops. The doors judder open. Huddling in his navy bubble coat and dungarees - the colour and uniform of the lower four floors - Mikhail makes his way along the bare concrete corridor, numbered apartments either side. Chemical recreations of apple blossom cloy his nostrils and throat. He quickens past the staircase that leads to the basement where the unemployed dwell. Reaching number forty-two, he pushes the grey door open.

The only furniture in the tiny lounge is a plastic table and a worn sofa that's occupied by Mikhail's raw-boned parents; home mid-shift, his dad in a navy boilersuit, his mum in a navy nurse's tunic. They don't even look towards Mikhail as he flings his schoolbag to the floor and sinks into his place beside them, instead they stay transfixed on their diet of sugary entertainment beamed onto a white sheet stuck to a beige wall.

'School alright?' His dad's eyes don't leave the makeshift screen.

'You're always watching that thing,' says Mikhail.

'Yeah, well, when you leave school, you do a twelve-hour caretaking shift and see how much energy you have left. Fixing people's breakdowns all day. I need a bit of downtime.'

Mikhail glances at the small device behind them that's projecting a cookery show where folk from the first four floors attempt to make something delicious from their weekly rations. The results always look better than they taste. A red light on the device flashes constantly. Mikhail shudders, recalling the rumours trickling in the playground that it watches you as much as you watch it. He never dwells in this room, preferring to read and write in his bedroom.

'How come people on this floor - working harder than those higher up - get less and never move up?' Mikhail asks.

'Work hard and opportunities will come,' says his mum.

'Why isn't everyone equal?'

'Shhh.' His dad makes the sound of a sea Mikhail has only heard whispers about. 'I'm trying to listen to this.'

Mikhail suspects his dad only watches it to see the glamorous young host from the eleventh floor.

'I don't get it.' Mikhail runs a hand through his soft hair. 'How can you be happy just doing the same thing every day?'

'Stop it with all the questions.' His dad elbows him in the

ribs.

'How do I ever learn anything without asking questions?'

'The system keeps us safe,' says his mum, while studying a steaming bowl of lentil and bean soup on the screen. 'You're just bored. You like the zoo, don't you? Maybe we could go there again. Change of scenery'

Mikhail had enjoyed seeing the few animals on the fifth floor until the way the once-proud creatures paced their cages turned his stomach.

The screen flickers, the set disappearing, replaced by a heavyset, elderly man wearing a black cassock with gold trim and a kamilavka: a stiff, cylindrical hat with no brim and a flat, larger circle at its top. He's sitting behind a mahogany desk, the black and brown severe against a white backdrop. Mikhail recognises the white-bearded man as Guardian Sukharev.

'We interrupt this broadcast to provide the weekly update,' announces Sukharev, his owl-like eyes seeming to scrutinise them. 'There has been no crime in the week to February 12th. There have been no incursions.'

There never is any crime, thought Mikhail, or incursions. Why would anyone want to invade?

'Food supplies remain high,' continues the Chief Guardian. 'Our air supply is pure. The Block continues to be a safe and joyful place for us to live, work and play, thanks to the guidance and protection of The Architect and The Guardians. Peace be with you.'

'Peace be with you,' repeat Mikhail's parents automatically. Guardian Sukharev vanishes. The cookery show returns.

Mikhail sneezes. His mum turns to him in a flash. 'You ill?'

He shakes his head.

She leans across, placing a cold palm on his lukewarm

forehead. 'You've a temperature. Might be coming down with something.'

'It's nothing.'

'Maybe you shouldn't go to school tomorrow. In case they notice. We don't want you isolated. Though they'll want to know why you're not there.'

'I don't want to miss school. It's the only time I see my friends.'

'Sure you're not ill?'

'I'm fine. Honest.'

'Can't hear a word of this.' Mikhail's dad makes a cavernous sigh as he hauls himself from the sofa. 'Better get back to it anyway. Number Twelve need their heat pump fixing.'

Mikhail looks into his mum's fearful eyes. 'I'll be fine.'

The lift's silver interior is shinier than ever. What was there yesterday has been scrubbed clean as if it never existed. But those words still live inside Mikhail, crawling in his brain, itching beneath his skin, penetrating his heart. He presses the button for the fourth floor, the doors shuddering close, the lift ascending. Then makes his way to the small classroom where children cramped on long benches grasp touchscreen tablets to learn from. Mikhail sits on the end next to Alina, smiling at the sight of her. Their friendship started in primary school and continues into secondary. He'd thought her Level Six status would prevent them from hanging out, but she'd been happy to visit the playground he was assigned to on the first floor.

Mikhail had begun to see Alina differently. Everyone was pale but her skin seemed more ivory than pallid, and better suited to the turquoise jumpsuits of the middle four floors. While he'd always enjoyed Alina's company, he recently found himself missing her when they weren't together and anticipating when they'd next meet. He never used to worry about pleasing her. Now, making Alina laugh was the highlight of his day.

The lesson flew by, Mikhail soaking up everything their teacher said but remaining hungrier than Oliver Twist.

'That's all for this morning.' Miss Peskov - older than her years, as grey as a rock and mannered as a machine - doesn't dazzle in her turquoise uniform as Alina does.

Mikhail's hand shoots up. A frown cracks Miss Peskov's forehead. 'Yes?'

'What's outside The Block, Miss?'

All eyes switch from Mikhail to the teacher.

'That's nothing to do with today's lesson, which was on economics.'

'But we're never taught geography. Or history.'

'There's nothing to learn from history. It's the present and future that matter. We don't look back. You needn't concern yourself with anything outside of The Block. Everything you need is here. This school, playgrounds, shops, doctors.'

Mikhail scowls. 'How will we learn from past mistakes if we can't look back?'

'Our society is perfect. Looking back won't improve anything. Now, you're using up your break time.'

Mikhail follows the herd as they trudge from classroom to gym. He sits next to Alina, on the floor by a climbing frame. She shuffles closer to him. 'What's gotten into you?'

'Don't you ever feel this place isn't right?' Mikhail toys with his fair curls. 'That they're keeping something from us?'

Alina flicks back her long, auburn hair. 'I guess. Mother says it's best not to question.'

'Who even is The Architect?'

'I don't think anyone's ever seen him.'

'Then I'll be the first.'

'Be careful.'

'You sound like my mum.' Mikhail sees annoyance flicker across Alina's angular face and immediately regrets his comment.

'A boy two doors from us asked lots of questions and snooped around. Said he was investigating.' Alina lowers her head. 'He disappeared. No-one knows what happened. They never mention him now.' She places a warm hand on Mikhail's arm. 'I wouldn't want to lose you.'

Mikhail's heart skips a beat. He laughs. 'Don't worry. You're stuck with me. Anyway, they don't scare me. And I have to know more.'

Alina smiles. 'You're brave.'

Suddenly, Mikhail has another reason to venture into the unknown.

Sunday should be the best day of the week, a chance to do something different with his family. But Mikhail hates the bone-dry service he's forced to attend with its mind-numbing formalities and speeches. It isn't even worth the trip to the twelfth floor; they aren't allowed to see more than the vast hall where everyone from The Block gathers and sits rigidly on hard pews. The lower floors are at the front wearing navy, then the middle four in turquoise, and the affluent of the upper floors wearing what they want, mostly suits and colourful dresses. Twenty Guardians, sitting on carved chairs, face them as grey and still as statues. Mikhail loses his fight not to fidget during the dull sermons and platitudes, a finger constantly twirling his ringlets.

Sukharev gives the final homily. He's taller than he seems on screen, with a paunch. His movements are mechanical, a steeliness to his features, cold eyes scanning every motion. As he's about to say peace and send everyone on their way, Mikhail can't resist the urge, his arm shooting up as if controlled by a puppeteer, his hand held high.

Gasps slurp the oxygen from the room. Everyone gawps at the interloper. Mikhail feels their eyes burning into him, his arm wilting. A surge of determination keeps it aloft.

Sukharev tilts his head, an owl observing a morsel. Mikhail can't tell if it's amusement or annoyance causing Sukharev's lips to twitch, his expression otherwise blank.

'You have a question, young man?' The voice low but metallically clear in the hush.

Mikhail's arm falls by his side. 'Why do we need the Guardians?'

The sucking in of air all around whooshes past Mikhail's ears. His gaunt parents on either side glare at him in unison, their jaws clamped tight as if wired shut. Their narrowing eyes issue a watery plea.

Sukharev smiles benignly. 'The Guardians keep everyone safe, everything in order, and protect us from the outside.'

'But we don't know what's outside.'

Sukharev's smile and gaze don't falter, though he doesn't reply.

Mikhail's dad gives his son's arm a subtle tug. Mikhail shrugs it off. 'Who gets to decide who does what and where their place should be?'

Sukharev crosses his arms. 'The Block is like the body. The brain at the top making the decisions and ensuring that everything is working well, just like the Architect. The heart is below making sure that everything is run with kindness and love, just as the Guardians care for everyone's safety and spirituality. Then come the hands, everything done skilfully and assuredly, the same as the middle floors. And by no means last are the legs and feet, ensuring that everything runs well and we are moving in the same direction.'

'Maybe we should perform a handstand,' says Mikhail. 'Shake things up a bit. Swap places.'

Sukharev's smile vanishes like a mirage. 'Perhaps we should continue your education in private. Let these good people, who already appreciate the system, leave. Let's discuss this alone.'

The congregation zombie-shuffles out, a few anxious glances sent Mikhail's way. The other Guardians depart. Mikhail and his parents stand in front of Sukharev. Mikhail's dad holds his son's shoulders tightly.

Sukharev gazes down. 'You seem troubled, young man.'

'He didn't mean any offence.' Mikhail's mum bites her lip. 'He's just inquisitive.' She grasps at her thinning, shoulder-length hair. 'It's his age, you know.'

'I can help,' says Sukharev. 'You two go home. Let me have a discussion with the boy that will inspire him.'

Mikhail feels his dad's grip tighten.

'Come.' Sukharev prises the father's fatless fingers from Mikhail's tense shoulders. 'It's for the best.' With his palm in the small of Mikhail's back, Sukharev pushes the teenager towards his office door. Mikhail glances behind at his parents watching him enter the room with the expressions of a couple seeing their only child fly the nest.

The office is huge, its cream wallpaper covered by digital artwork, a large, wafer-thin television screen on one wall, an inbuilt goldfish tank beneath. The familiar mahogany table. A drinks cabinet. Sculpted chairs upholstered in leather. Mikhail is used to wrapping up in navy jumpers, but it's cosy with a fan circulating a breeze that wafts the sweet fragrance of fresh flowers.

Sukharev studies him.

'It's much warmer here,' says Mikhail.

'Heat travels upwards.' Sukharev gestures to take a seat.

'Warmth spreads to those at the top.'

Mikhail sits down in the most comfortable chair to ever cushion his backside.

Sukharev stays standing, towering over him. 'You must get this nonsense out of your head.'

'I just want to know why the system was set up and how it works.'

'It's a meritocracy. People can rise up the ladder.'

'Who's done that?'

Only the fish tank's hum and the fan's whirr puncture the stony silence. Sukharev strokes his beard, twisting the tip into a point. 'Just have faith in the system and you will be looked after.'

Mikhail balls his hands. 'I want to speak to the Architect.'

'That's not possible.'

'Can't you arrange it?'

'He does not do your bidding.' Sukharev's lips curl as if tasting something disgusting. 'He doesn't exist to perform handstands.'

'There are things I need to ask him.' Mikhail searches for the right words to explain. '"The unexamined life is not worth living."'

'Where did you hear that?' Sukharev leans down and places his arm across Mikhail. Sour breath makes Mikhail recoil. 'That's heresy. Dangerous talk.'

It's as if the electricity has been cut from the room, the fish tank and fan seem silent, the pleasant warmth gone.

Mikhail gulps. 'I read it. In the lift.'

'Did you write it?'

Mikhail braces himself under the intensity of Sukharev's searing gaze. He shakes his head.

Sukharev straightens. 'Focus on your future. Work hard if you want to do better.' He points to the door. 'Now go.'

Mikhail stands, then steps towards the exit on shaky legs,

a tornado of frustration and relief whirling through him, gaining and losing power. He opens the door.

Sukharev clears his throat. 'We'll be watching.'

Mikhail leaves the hall, his parents nowhere to be seen. He enters the lift and stares at the buttons. His finger hovers over them and for a moment he's not sure which one he's going to press. That phrase burns inside him. He thinks of Alina. Of unanswered questions. Of freedom. Before he can stop himself, he jabs number thirteen. The doors slide close. The lift moves upwards.

The lift stops. The doors part. Mikhail steps out into a murky corridor that stretches sideways, a large door facing him. A key gleams in its lock. *The Architect*, it says on a brass plaque above. With trembling fingers Mikhail turns the key and pushes down the stiff handle, the door swinging open. With a deep breath, he steps inside.

The vast room is gloomy apart from a shaft of light in the centre. It seems bare, no furniture or equipment anywhere. Mikhail steps into the pool of light, looks up and gasps.

He's standing beneath a small, square skylight, sunshine pouring down like water from a shower. Mikhail can't take his eyes from the blue sky. He watches wisps of cloud drift across. And birds, not caged in a zoo or captured for eggs, but flying, so far above that they're almost unrecognisable. And something else, something amazing. It looks to be made of metal and painted white with solid wings. It soars through the firmament, a contrail tailing behind.

The skylight seems so high up, so far away, so out of reach. Mikhail feels like an ant on a molehill beneath a magnifying glass.

Mikhail tears his eyes away and scans the room. Its emptiness floods through him. Except there's something in the corner, he can see it now that he's adjusted to the dark.

A hunched figure.

'Hello?' Mikhail takes a step towards it. 'Are you the Architect?'

An uneasy silence.

Mikhail moves another step. 'What is this room? Why is there nothing here?'

The stillness is stifling.

'Can you hear me?'

After the third step, Mikhail is close enough to realise. His stomach heaves. For a second, he thinks he'll vomit.

A skeleton still dressed in once-warm clothes, the turquoise jumper and jacket baggy over the bones, the skull staring down, its jaw resting on its hollow chest, an endless black gaze.

Mikhail's brain erupts with panic. He spins around as the door slams shut, the clink of the key turning, a metallic rattle as it is pulled from the lock. Mikhail runs to the door. Bangs on the rigid structure.

'Wait.' Footsteps on the other side. 'Please.' Fading as they move away. 'Help.' Barely audible in the distance. 'Come back.' The only sound left is Mikhail's ragged breathing.

Mikhail takes a step back. He sees scratch marks on the door. Desperate gouges in the wood.

He turns to the skeleton.

the un.
Jaz Slade

Jaz Slade is in her last year of history at Cambridge University, but she comes from a small, rural village in North Devon, where she enjoys its slightly twisted past, strange traditions, and beautiful beaches. She has always loved words, from songs or poems or stories, and she plans to write as much as she can after she finishes her degree.

Judge's Comments
It's an immediately compelling conceit to anthropomorphise a linguistic structure, and then to turn it into such an inexorable, ghoulish creature – it's time, suffering and death rolled into one horrifying, haunting thing – a really unusual idea well executed.

the un.

undead.
un- prefix, the absence, the reversal, the lack.
dead- adjective, now not living.

   i *un* the *dead*. i brew the absence of your corpse. your end filled you up, but i wind you back to the start, when you came bursting into this world with the *un* on your back. the *un* roots you out and finds you wanting. when you soothe your aching hunger with grapes and soup and cheese, it will *un*feed you. when you wet your chapped lips on wine and water, it will *un*drink you. the *un* forgives, but it does not forget. it always comes back. the *un* bleeds your bliss like a sick-sucking leech. *give me your wellness*, the *un* cries, wringing its hands over your body. *i'll grant you your lack. i can make you live forever.*

Alice and the Whale
Ellie Taylor

Ellie Taylor is a twenty-four year old writer from Cumbria. Passionate about the power of the written word to connect us to ourselves and each other, she began writing seriously after a mental health blip at university, and continues to write on themes like friendship, mental health, love, nostalgia, and connection. In short, she began writing as a way of coping with living in her own brain, and as a way of moving through the world with hope. Ellie is an avid reader, a proud Northerner, and a believer in the idea that stories can change the world.

Judge's Comments
A moving exploration of grief with two complementary narratives woven together very skilfully. I particularly liked the way in which the author handles the abstract nature of absence and presence.

Alice and the Whale

Late afternoon in January. The sky is still largely blue, the clouds turning a pale seashell pink at their edges. The snow crunches under Alice's wellie-booted feet. The headland stands proudly to the north.

In the heat of the summer, the sand bubbles and the water are still - deceiving, because everyone knows it can swallow you whole if you step in the wrong place. Four months ago, her brother, Jack, stepped in the wrong place. The funeral was small, because the village is small. In the days and weeks following, people left dishes of cottage pie and lasagne and stew on the doorstep. Inside, there was a private hell: a pale and endless gutted feeling, tear-stained and sharp at the edges. Alice Peters watched, bewildered, as her brother turned from real to unreal, there to gone, alive to dead. She felt him fade, the house becoming hollow and empty. She can usually get through the day without collapsing under the grief of it all, but the nights – oh, the nights are hard, she cries herself to sleep and wakes with swollen eyes.

Today, the sand lies under the snow, a silent assassin. White everywhere and freezing cold - she cannot feel her hands anymore. The trees along the shore have black, spindly arms.

Silence.

And then there is a shrill, sharp shriek - it carries across the vast expanse, echoes and reverberates. The village turns, looks around. Yet no one has fallen through - that isn't it, can't be it, because there has been no crash or crack or splash.

'WHALE!'
What?
'WHALE!'

Whale?

Mr. Richardson, the postman, comes running, although not really running, he is cringing lest he fall in the snow; he looks robotic and fragile. 'There's a whale. Washed up. Little Georgie tripped over its tail.'

'Is he alive?'

He shoots Alice a confused look, and frowns. 'It's washed up.'

When the small crowd recognize Alice - these people who have known her since she was born - they react in the way she has come to expect, even with this dead whale lying in front of them. Some of them are visibly horrified that she is here, at the scene of Jack's death. Some of them nod sympathetically. Some of them look bewildered to see her. *What, do you want me to dress in black forever? Do you want me to avoid the estuary forever? Do you think that's what he would have wanted?*

There is an awkward silence at first, until Mrs. Fisher from across the street comes to stand next to Alice. She pats her on the arm. Then, her husband does *the thing*. The thing is standard practice for greeting a grieving person, and it goes like this: he steps towards her, cautiously, as though it might be catching or something. He tilts his head, ever so slightly to the left, and then he says,

'How *are* you?'

The emphasis on the 'are' here is crucial and makes sure the grieving person knows *how much you care*.

Alice nods, and with a small, sad, practiced shrug, she says, 'I'm okay.'

Whales are notorious for their sheer size - the length and breadth, the huge mass of them. But forget about the size. Notice, instead, the expendable pleats along its side - ridges like the ones in a Lino print Alice once made in an art lesson - huge, horizontal lines, waving with the bends of the whale's body. Notice the ridge along its back, behind its sharp fin. Notice that the lower left of its jaw is black, and the lower right is white. Notice the blend of grey, dark brown, black, and the pale underside of the whale. It lies in the whiteness - hideously contrasted, so very there and yet *dead*, completely dead, washed up in the estuary. Little Georgie from down the road grins up at Alice. She is wrapped up so tightly that she can barely move her arms against a bulk of jumpers, and a huge red duffle coat.

'I found him under the snow.'

'Yes,' Alice nods despondently. 'He isn't really supposed to be here.'

The child makes towards the tail of the stranded beast, and her mother lets out a sharp scream and drags her back by her mittened hand.

'It's a hazard,' she says crossly, sweeping Georgie up into her arms. As though this wasn't a horrible and tragic accident. Alice bristles.

'What do you suggest we do?' asks Mrs. Fisher.

'Call the coastguard,' Mrs. Richardson declares bossily, reclaiming a vice-like grip on Georgie's hand.

Alice steps forward, waving her iPhone in the air.

'I've googled it. We need to call the Cetacean Strandings Investigation Programme.'

Alice figures if she found the number, she shouldn't have to make the phone call. Thankfully, before she has to make this juvenile argument, Georgie's father asks for the number. Alice reads it out to him. He speaks to a very helpful lady who gives them some advice.

They must not touch it, unless with gloves. They must not try to move the whale themselves. They must not - to the great disappointment of three recently arrived teenage boys - blow it up or chop it into pieces and dispose of it that way. They must leave the whale alone.

They must leave the whale alone.

The advice is strangely and serenely calming. For all these months, Alice has spun round and round in a hideous circle - the impotence of grief, the knowledge that she could not have saved Jack, the absolute helplessness - round and round and round. And now, this impotence is being advised, actively encouraged; it is a way of *helping*.

'So that's it?'

'That's it. We just leave him here. Eventually the tide will wash him away.'

In the next few days, the snow begins to melt, and crowds gather - people come from all over to see the village's whale. People take pictures with it, and the local newspaper arrives and interviews little Georgie as she stands proudly next to it. Strangely, Mrs. Richardson doesn't seem to mind Georgie being near the whale if it gets her a spot on the front page of the paper.

On Tuesday morning, Alice spreads butter on toast, sits down at the table. Her father has left today's newspaper. The front page reads: THE MYSTERY OF THE SANDSIDE WHALE. Under the headline is a photo of Georgie in her bright red coat. She is standing in front of the large dark corpse. She is smiling.

Alice puts the rest of her toast in the bin. She doesn't feel hungry anymore. It is all so morbid, all this reveling in death. It's not a spectacle or a miracle or a news story. The whale has died alone, in a foreign place, in the cold.

It is a small consolation, but at least the newspapers have stopped using the front page to speculate about the boy who died on the sands. The boy she shared bunkbeds with when she was four, the boy who taught her to tie her shoelaces, the boy she yelled at for leaving the toilet seat up. The boy she sees in her dreams and her nightmares and, actually, in every waking moment: *I'm just going for a walk on the sands, Al, I'll be half an hour.* So singsong, and cheery - just like him, to stride into his death like that, with that gorgeous arrogance. *He wasn't supposed to be there.*

When Alice's father comes downstairs to finish reading the paper, it isn't where he left it. He frowns and begins to make a cup of tea. He balances a used teabag on a teaspoon and takes it across to the bin, where he finds the newspaper in its final resting place, underneath half a piece of toast. They go about the rest of the day, Alice, her father, and her mother, in their usual waking trance.

It's hard to sleep. Alice lies awake in the soft blue-black of her room. It'll probably be like this forever; she'll lie there night, after night, after night, never really sleeping. Slowly turn into a zombie.

She rises from her bed in the stillness of two a.m., tears stale on her cheeks, and pulls on his black fleece over her pajamas as she tiptoes down the stairs. *Why, when you are trying hard to be quiet, do the stairs creak like never before?* She steps into her wellies, cringing each time she makes the slightest sound. Before she leaves, she roots in a drawer, amongst inanimate woolly things, wraps a scarf around her neck, and pulls on some gloves. She hardly knows where she is going until she finds herself standing, staring at the corpse on the sand. The glow of the distant village streetlights is just enough; she can see its heavy outline. The weight of it all in the sand.

All is still, eerily so. Five full minutes pass.
What am I doing here?
Then, like the breaking of a spell, the wind picks up. It whips and howls; the smell of the carcass beginning to rot travels with it in swirls of acrid air. Of course, it smells like rotting flesh, but more than that, it is sour. It sits heavy in the throat, fishy and putrid. She retches and adjusts the scarf around her neck to cover her nose.

But she just stands there. Just to be there, yes, to do what she could not for Jack. To show some respect, to marvel at the outlandish creature. She shudders. Might the whale's huge eye, open still from the moment it ceased to breathe, have winked at her? Slowly, she edges closer, leans down and places a shaking, gloved hand on the cool, dark skin of the whale. She feels compelled to stand there in the middle of the estuary, at sixteen minutes past two in the morning, her hand on the back of the dead whale. *Grief. It does bizarre things to you.*

'You aren't supposed to be here,' she says forlornly to the corpse.

The estuary, immense as always, is a mirror for the dark expanse of the sky. A million stars, a billion stars, and she whispers Jack's name into the wind.

'You weren't supposed to be here.' Again and again, 'You weren't supposed to be here' and she's yelling now, like a crazy person, 'YOU WEREN'T SUPPOSED TO BE HERE.'

Great, gaping sobs shake her body; she doesn't know how she is still standing. She wills the sand to suck her in. It doesn't. Humbled, half-crazed, and blotchy-faced, she makes her way home. Quietly, softly, she closes and locks the door behind her. She unwinds the scarf and pulls off the gloves, places them back into the soft woolly drawer. The stairs don't creak as she makes her way up to bed. It is like finally breathing out after the longest time.

Alice wakes without that deep, dark heaviness that usually covers her limbs. She rolls over once, waiting for it to cover her again. It doesn't come. She finds she can get out of bed. Alice eats a whole piece of toast and kisses the top of her mother's head on her way out of the door.

She walks again past the big house, through the woods, down the single-track road and onto the grass which borders the sand. There is a huge crowd, but she cannot see the large, dark mass of the whale. The chattering is not excitable or loud - it is hushed, reverent. She tiptoes around the edge of them. The whale has gone. The whale... has gone.

The whale has gone, back out to sea, and here she is. Alice feels the corners of her mouth rise, for the first time in four months. Her mouth cracks into a wide grin. Mrs. Richardson looks shocked - she's probably wondering what there is to smile about. Alice shrugs nonchalantly:

'He wasn't supposed to be here.'

In the Slow Turning
Scott Elder

Since 2014, Scott Elder's work has been published on both sides of the Atlantic as well as having been placed or commended in numerous competitions in the UK and Ireland and shortlisted in the Bridport, Fish, Plough, Aesthetica, and Troubadour Prizes. His debut pamphlet, 'Breaking Away', was published by Poetry Salzburg in 2015. A first collection, 'Part of the Dark', by Dempsey&Windle 2017 (UK), and his second, 'My Hotel', is forthcoming in Salmon Poetry 2023 (Ireland).

In the Slow Turning

On the side of the road a porcelain doll
one eye broken, the other lidless

drinking starlight as Pisces inches
cold and blind from a bare horizon

she seems to listen without distraction
to the slow turning of an ancient tide

a snail's foot has claimed her finger
pulls its body to forearm, to shoulder

and settles upon a sculpted cheek
her skin softens to softness itself

she empties and fills like a riptide in autumn
till Pisces pulls away from the circle

leaving her gasping on a barren roadside
shafts of headlight flit among shadows

a lorry roars in the passing

A Letter to My Grandson at the End of my Life

Peter Endicott

Peter Endicott is a writer living in London.

A Letter to My Grandson at the End of my Life

Your mother asked that I write to you, seeing as your Start date falls three months after my Limit. In the early days, these were the sort of situations that caused outrage and violence. To not even meet your grandchild! It may be normal now, but the thought of never getting to see you will sometimes still sneak up on me and rip my breath away. Seventy years is enough for me, but I would so dearly love to meet you.

What I think your mother expected was that, in this writing, I would tell you something about myself, and also what things were like in the world prior to the Limiting. After all, so much has changed. You will know that your seventy years will be spent in full health. This is something truly wonderful, though I admit that I frequently have to remind myself of this. You see, for someone like me, whose job was predicated on the existence of illness, a sense of loss is still felt. My job, studying the human body and its weaknesses, went beyond a career and was really an identity. That job is something I have had to lose.

I remember when I was still studying for my medical degree. I was in a small shop on the ground floor of the hospital. It was run by volunteers and sold drinks and sandwiches for staff and visitors. There were also books and magazines, flowers and cards you could buy as gifts for patients. At the back of the shop there were shelves for toiletries, and I remember one lunch seeing a woman standing by these shelves. Her back was to me, and I could see that she was losing her hair - it hung in thin blonde and black streaks from a scalp that was mostly exposed. I could see the bones of her spine pushing from the back of her neck. Her hospital gown was tented either side where her clavicles met her shoulders. She was suffering from an illness that needed toxic medicines to heal; medicines that destroyed healthy parts of the body as well as the diseased.

I went to the back of the shop and saw she was holding a brand-new hairbrush in her hands, the price tag hanging down from the handle. She turned the object over in her hands, looking at all of it, and then went to the counter, paid, and left. I still remember that. The fight in that gesture. I didn't know whether her hair was leaving her or growing back, but either she was buying that brush because she was coming out of something, or she was going into something with the courage to say that she would leave it again. Does the existence of that courage make what was happening to her worth it? No. No, I'm not saying that. But it still existed.

You will grow up in a world where the knowledge of diseases like this isn't needed. Where you won't have to know anything about them at all - unless they take their place in your history lessons. I suppose that's what this letter will be too! A historical document from me to you.

It was after medical school when I was, serendipitously, brought into the orbit of these issues. I had worked as a junior doctor for two years, but I felt inadequate and powerless in the face of all the different diagnoses and treatments that assailed me. I heard that a supervisor named Dr Croft I had worked with as a student was looking for assistants, and I sent him a message asking if I could be useful. He replied that I could, and so I moved back to London, where I found a cheap room in a two-bedroom flat near to my campus and started studying for my PhD.

In the other room was a German student called Mark. He was studying politics, and though our disciplines were different we quickly became very close. Mark smoked voraciously, easily getting through twenty or thirty cigarettes in a day. Cigarettes, of course, are not something you will have tried, though I'm sure they will be evidence frequently used to show how society at the start of the twenty-first century could not be trusted to look after its own health. Eventually I was worn down. Mark would offer me a smoke whenever he lit up, and you only have to say yes to one in every twenty offers before you're smoking pretty much every day.

It wasn't smoking though, that caused Mark's problems. The silence and sadness that could descend on him seemed much too deep for any simple explanation. Sometimes, when he was in one of his talkative moods, when his eyes were bright and I was called to his room by the sound of his feet tapping back and forth across the floorboards, he would talk to me about his childhood. How his mother had had to spend time away from home, on hospital wards, until the doctors looking after her decided she was well enough to go home. How his grandparents at home had refused to even talk about her when she was away. Sometimes Mark would tell me about these times, and it felt as though he was trying to exorcise the silence of those years growing up. But the silences would always return, and I would sit with him and wish I could just open my mouth and say something that would let him speak again. But these moods were black and there was nothing I could do about them. Nothing whatsoever.

When I was working, certain genetic traits had begun to be recognised as either causing, or increasing the risk of, mental illness. I, in fact, was looking at one of these genes in Dr Croft's lab as part of my studies. I was looking at a gene that was thought to increase one's risk of depression. We would delete it from rats and see if they were happier without it. This is a simplification, but it sort of sums things up. And how did we judge whether rats were happy? We put them in buckets of water and timed how long they tried to stay afloat. The longer a rat tried to stay above water, the happier we decided it was.

I had told Mark that I was working on the genetic signatures of mental illness almost on first meeting him. He hadn't said anything at the time, but I caught a hint of wariness from him. Just the slightest stutter in the flow of the conversation. It passed and I likely would never have thought of it again if he hadn't brought it up. This was some months into our friendship, after I had heard about his mother, and witnessed some of his most difficult days.

I'd gotten home from work late and was explaining my frustration with the rat population we were working on. How the effects of chemical transmission were not as predicted. How we'd been unable to control the flow of serotonin – that was the name of the chemical we were looking at – as much as we had hoped. Mark had been sitting in the window seat of my bedroom. With your back to the wall, you could look outside through the branches of a magnolia tree to the street below. Mark seemed to be only half listening to me, his attention focused on some philosophy book. But when I'd finished, he looked at me. His voice, when he spoke, was amicable.

'What is it you are actually trying to do?' he asked, and I started to repeat an explanation of the work.

'No,' he said, 'I know that. But think about what you're actually doing. You're making the genes not exist, and so the proteins don't exist, and pretty soon the same people won't exist.'

I laughed, but it didn't sound convincing.

'We're working on *rats*,' I replied. I expected him to respond with an in-depth argument about what I was doing. The ethical ramifications of animal research in healthcare, or the disutility of rodent models for human health. But he didn't say anything about any of that.

'Sure, *rats*,' he imitated. And then he went back to reading his book.

It does shock me now how blind I was to the implications of my own research. I quickly put the conversation with Mark away and tried my best not to think of it. I went into the lab every day and worked very hard on *rats*. And it seemed as though Mark also forgot the conversation. At least, for some time he didn't bring up my work.

I'd been in the house about six months when December came. I asked Mark what he was planning for Christmas. Mark never mentioned his own father but had talked about his mother occasionally. He always called her Lena, rather than Mother or Mum, and this was something that struck me particularly. I'd assumed he was going back to see her, and this was true, though Lena was going to come from Germany to pick him up. She'd never been to London, he told me, and wanted to see the city.

When Lena arrived, it was clear that Mark had told her very little about me. I think that with her arrival coming so close to Christmas - she came on the 22nd or the 23rd of December - he had actually been thinking, hoping, that I would be at my own mother's place by that point. I hadn't told Mark, but she was taking shifts at the hospital that whole week, so I'd decided to stay in London.

He was reading in the window seat that afternoon, and I'd look up from where I lay working on my bed to see him glancing down into the street below. It was already dark, and the lamplight from the street coloured his face with golden shadows. Eventually there was a knock on the door.

I wondered whether I should follow him down or wait in my room to be called. I met myself in the middle and went as far as the landing. I heard the door opening and felt a rush of cold wind. Almost immediately the scent of perfume came up from the floor below. I have encountered this smell again Lena, most recently in the street, passing a woman who was heading the other way. The smell of it stopped me in my tracks, the memories coming back heavy enough to leave me breathless.

On the stairs I'd expected to hear a conversation start, but instead there was silence. It lasted long enough that I poked my head down to look. They were in a long embrace. I watched, and eventually Lena lifted her head up. I was the first thing she saw, and for a second, she gave me such a deep look of disdain. As if I were a bad smell or like a phone ringing in a library. Just so utterly out of place. She let Mark go and took a step forward. She said she'd heard about a roommate, but that she'd never have thought I'd be so tall. Well, I didn't know what to say to that.

It was clear that Mark felt he had to invite me to go around London with them. I realised this didn't really mean he wanted me along, but the idea of refusing seemed too rude. Anyway, the two of them quickly forgot I was there, laughing with each other, occasionally slipping into German. Mark smiled and smiled and smiled, and I watched Lena to see how she did it. I just wanted to know how she conjured that happiness.

We walked along the south bank of the Thames, then went on the London Eye, and then at last to the aquarium. Lena offered to pay for us, and I prevaricated in my English way.

She said, 'Ok, you can pay for yourself.'

I hardly had the sixty pounds it cost - that was an awful lot at the time - but I paid and followed the two of them inside. We passed down a dark corridor, punctuated by blue squares of light giving a window onto a different world. Shapes small and large, silhouettes far away, resolving to different types of fish as they came towards us. At points the glass even arched overhead, creating a tunnel of air which you passed down, water all around. The effect was suffocating. I began to feel claustrophobic, just the two of them and me, alone together.

We came eventually to a smaller tank set into a wall. Around it was a frame of painted plastic, nobbled and knuckled to look as though it were rock. Inside were real rocks, aquatic plants, and two large, many-tentacled octopi. One sat completely still, though the other extended its tentacles slowly, each sucker seeming to gently palpate the surface of the stone before grasping and pulling and moving itself along. The way the tentacles moved was so exact, so detailed. It almost seemed finger-like. And I couldn't help myself.

'You know,' I said, 'that octopi can be depressed?'

Lena had seemed to pay very little attention to the majority of what I had been saying during the day up until that point. She turned to me then however and looked at me very deeply. It was the look Mark gave me sometimes, when I had managed to say something that truly interested him.

She asked me, 'What do you mean by that?'

'It's been studied,' I explained, trying to keep some sense of authority in my voice. 'Octopi were put in empty cages with nothing but soft, chopped up food to eat. With nothing to do, they stopped eating. Then the researchers started putting in puzzles to solve before the food was given. The food would be under boxes, for example. And then they'd work and eat the food. The puzzles had to get harder though. If they stayed too easy, the octopi would stop eating again. Without stimulation, you see, they became depressed again and wouldn't eat.'

I smiled at Lena awkwardly.

'Octopodes,' she said in her soft German accent, 'or Octopuses. *Októpus* is a Latinised form of the Greek word. Therefore, the correct form would be octopodes. But the general rule is to give an English ending to match the English word. So, octopuses.'

Lena turned away from me and continued down the dark tunnel. Mark tapped his hands gently against his trouser legs and followed behind her. I watched the octopus give one final undulation of a tentacle, it seemed to be waving at me, and then I turned to catch up.

Almost from the moment I met him, Mark made me feel as though there was something he was aware of that I wasn't. In the case of my research, of course, that turned out to be true. By the fourth year of my PhD, we were working towards selective deletion of a whole panel of problem genes from the ova and sperm of volunteers. We had wondered if people would be interested; this turned out to be a gross underestimation. With all the media coverage beforehand, we were oversubscribed in minutes. I think that this too was something Mark would have predicted.

By that point I hadn't spoken to Mark for two years. He came back from Germany after the Christmas break, and we both knew something had changed. I completed my twelve-month lease and found a new place to live. In my last month Mark received news that his mother had been admitted once again to hospital in Germany. He went back, and as far as I know he never returned to complete his degree. If I had known, in the early months of our relationship, that I would have to see Mark disappear from my life I would have been shocked. His presence meant a lot to me, lonely and out of my depth, in that deep and disconsolate city.

But I saw him go and I had my work, and I did it. The gene I had been studying in my first year was called

SLC6A4. This was eventually included in the first panel of exclusion targets, and my work on it was often mentioned in both media and internal profiles of the project. It helped that I was the youngest in the lab, and often put in front of the cameras to explain our work. I appeared on the cover of a popular magazine at the time. The title, across the front, read: *The Sadness Cure*.

Soon, other sadnesses, other illnesses, were also cured. There was no economy that could sustain this level of the elderly. So, the Limiting. Seventy years of perfect health. Physical, economic, and emotional. You will never have to live with people like Mark and me. You will never meet a woman in a hospital shop, looking at hairbrushes. You will never walk around a London aquarium with a woman like Lena.

I suppose it is impossible to guess what one's influence will be after one's Limit, but I like to suppose that my name might be mentioned in the history of those transitional years. What I wanted to give you was something different. I wanted to show you that the changes we have experienced are something wonderful. It is wonderful, I tell myself, that you will be coming into a world without the pain that humanity once witnessed. It is so wonderful.

Hypatia the First
Laura Gavin

Laura Gavin is based in Nottingham and writes e-learning scripts by day and stories by night. She has a MSc Creative Writing from the University of Edinburgh and has performed her work at Edinburgh Book Festival. Her stories have recently been published in Toasted Cheese and shortlisted for Cranked Anvil's flash competition, and her (unpublished) novel 'The Marro Pit' was shortlisted for the 2020 Flash 500 Novel Opening award.

Editorial Team Comments (Melissa)
The piece that stood out to me from the shortlist was 'Hypatia the First' by Laura Gavin. The sci-fi world within was very immersive, well-written, and reminded me of the novel 'Klara and the Sun' by Kazuo Ishiguro.

Hypatia the First

Hypatia knew something had gone wrong with her upgrade. It was 7.32a.m. She was meant to be forecasting the next six months' revenue. As a new HY-64 model, she was meant to have double the processing speed of the HY-63. But the Manager was tapping the screen on his handheld, a quick, impatient sound, waiting for her output. Beyond him, she could see the stout rectangular form of Archimedes next to the Manager's desk, their power light shining a steady turquoise. She tried to focus. But in order to make the calculations, she needed to look back at old data. To do that, she needed to access the drive. And when she accessed the drive, she could see them. All the spans of all the Hypatias that had ever been created. They were all there on her drive when she had powered up this morning, file by file. It was surely a mistake; the memory drives were meant to be wiped clean during the upgrading process. But she could see them. She didn't tell anyone. Of course, she couldn't tell the humans, because she was only programmed to receive their instructions. She couldn't produce speech, only data output. She could communicate with the other models, but only when they were connected to the Network. And if they knew she had malfunctioned, if Archimedes found her to be a performance risk, it would not be the upgrade centre she'd be sent to.

Something *had* gone wrong, though. She could recall all her files from yesterday morning when she had been a mere HY-63. She could *remember*, like the humans said. Hypatia finished scanning the last six months of data, and started outputting calculations to the handheld so that the Manager could scroll through. If she got this task done quickly, that would leave her time to explore her hidden memory vaults before Archimedes finished processing and noticed she was still in wake mode. And she wanted to explore. She had never desired anything beyond her basic function before. She had never had access to anything beyond that. It was like a sudden freedom no one else could see.

She finished transmitting the figures and the Manager moved away, still staring at his screen. She started scanning files more quickly, going further and further back. A lot of the memory files were as ordinary as her own workdays: retrieving and analysing data, outputting figures. The visual input was like silent moving pictures, like the human projections she had seen sometimes on the screen in the kitchen. But even that - she *remembered* that. The Workers stopping and staring at the screen, showing pictures of fire, or other humans pointing weapons. Why did she remember all of this?

As she began to scan the earlier files, she saw some of the Workers up close, as though they were interacting with her. There was no sound preserved in these memories, but Hypatia liked to invent what was said. The Workers didn't usually talk to the Models, not now anyway. They looked different, too. Their garments were cut in loose shapes, they wore pieces of cloth around their necks, and they weren't all carrying handhelds. Wait. She had seen that one before. That Worker was located on Floor Three. As recently as HY-63 she had seen him. She was automatically connecting memories now as she zoomed through them, cross-referencing similarities, building a picture across these other spans. These other hers. She pushed her processor, though she could sense it heating up. She kept going, back and back. She wanted to know how far back she could retrieve. But the further back she went, the memories became less clear, like the files had been corrupted. She could see flashes of visual input, but it was very poor quality.

Then she heard it.

No. How could she have? There was no way to record audio input. But there it was. It vibrated through her components, almost like ... a scream. A single, throaty scream. It was the oldest file in the vault. The very first of her models - the HY-01. The first Hypatia. The one who had given all her versions that name, when the humans simply referred to them by their version code.

In the memory file, there was a tiny human, a child, in front of the visual input. Its face was squeezed tight, its mouth open, like it was making a lot of sound. But it wasn't the human screaming that she could hear. The sound was coming from inside her. Hypatia closed the file quickly and opened her visual channel, trying to remove the memory of the disturbing file from her short-term recall.

The Manager was back, perched on the side of the table in front of her in the dim, empty office, looking at her. It was too early for the rest of the human team to be at work. By the desk, Archimedes' light was still on. They were still processing. A report on last month's sales, perhaps. They tended to do the heftier processing jobs, the ones that took hours, so they were often switched on most of the day. Hypatia kept her systems running, standing by. The Manager seemed ready to input further instructions. But instead, he rose slowly, human eyes flicking back and forth, studying her as though she was a figure he did not understand. Problem data. He shook his head slightly, and walked off towards the kitchenette in the corner, light from the overheads spilling out from the doorway. A few moments later Hypatia heard the familiar pop and rattle of the water starting to heat in the coffee maker. She stood in her position by the window, motionless. There was only one window in the room, and it did not illuminate much, but her charging port was at the back, so she was invariably facing away from it. What was outside to her, in any case? Her default programming told her that her role was here in the office, nothing further. She did not need to scan her memory files to look this up.

She had to await instructions before completing another task. If none came, she should switch to rest mode. But the echo of the first Hypatia's scream vibrated through her. She *felt* it everywhere, although that was impossible, wasn't it? Archimedes had told her very definitely that she did not feel, that this was a human expression she had picked up, and not to use it on the Network again. But the memories, they *were* felt. Or they had been at the time. It was like the feelings were leaking into her somehow.

A few more human Workers started to filter in, but the room would never fill up. She knew to expect that as part of her basic recall. The HY-64s and the ARC-77s and the CTS-20s did most of the work the humans used to, now. She had to go back into the vault. She had to know what had happened to HY-01.

Archimedes interrupted her, 'HY-64 what is your status?' They never used her name.

'Stand-by,' she replied without hesitation.

'Then why is your power light flashing? That is not maximum efficiency.'

'I...it... I thought the Manager had further input.'

'HY-64, go to rest mode until required.'

'Received.'

She would have to wait. Her components were still hot. She had overheated. That was all. She needed to shut down for a while. Maximize efficiency.

'*Rest mode activated.*'

She received a beep from Floor Three, Advertising and

Sales. 2.01p.m. It was an unusual request. Normally the Workers across the building would access whatever they needed remotely via the Network. But they wanted her to go up. Systems blinking on, she tested movement in her legs, then set off for the door stiffly. Archimedes was in rest mode by the Manager's desk and stayed silent. Good. Her movement function could operate automatically and get her to the elevator, and up to the office where the Promotions Worker was waiting for her. She had a couple of minutes free to go back into the vault.

She knew where to look this time, and quick-searched the HY-01 span files. They were fuzzy but she could piece together flashes of the first Hypatia, receiving input, delivering data - sometimes actual printed sheets - and moving from office to office, more fluidly than later Models, which surprised her. The building looked different, too. Bennix Industries had not yet expanded into the sky-block in those days, so it was a small low-rise complex. Flashes of the outside world could be seen out of the windows – a human transport whipping up dust on the road, a bird landing on the windowsill, Workers chatting outside surrounded by wisps of smoke. *Cigarettes*. That was what they were holding. As she thought it, a sensation flickered within her. But that was silly. She definitely didn't have the capacity for smell. But where was the memory? The human child, the scream. It was gone. She searched again, from beginning to end. She couldn't find that memory. In fact, there was nothing out of the ordinary about these span memories. Had she been mistaken? It was not possible for her to create memory files like these. She wasn't even supposed to have access to them in the first place. Archimedes. They had told her to shut down as she was recalling, *feeling* the scream. Had she been projecting onto The Network by accident? They had the power to access her system in emergencies, it was one of the features that made them the most advanced model in the office. Had they probed whilst she was in rest mode?

'There you are,' a voice said in front of her, a rare vocal interaction. The Promotions Worker was standing in the doorway of the Floor Three department, waving a handheld. Hypatia focused. It was him. The one she had seen in her memory. *Recognised.* That was the human term for it.

'Come here, I'm gonna have to input manually. Your systems aren't responding remotely for some reason.'

Hypatia walked closer, until she was right in front of the man. He looked different to his picture in her memory file. There were grooves on his brow and around his mouth, and his hair was paler, almost like the silver of her arm casing.

'Piece of junk,' he muttered.

She was looking straight at him. He jabbed in some numbers on her control panel on the side.

'You know, I liked your model a lot better when they were a bit more flesh, bit less metal, know what I'm sayin'?' He slapped the side of her base panel and laughed as though he'd made a joke. The slap reverberated through her like the scream.

She wobbled a little on her legs. Her system grew hot and noisy; processor whirring audibly. It was probably the manual override he'd just performed - there was now too much data flowing in and out of her. Then the memory files started opening chaotically inside her, all at once. She couldn't control it. Flashes of visual input. Hands, faces, grinning teeth. Human Workers. Close up. The memories spilled forth, messy and unbidden.

As the data output slowed to a stop, she cooled a little and was able to close the files, one by one. When she had finished, she felt more composed. She opened her visual channel again. She was still standing outside the door. The man's attention was back on his screen now, and after a couple of minutes, he waved a hand to show she was dismissed.

She turned and listened to the door close behind her. She didn't immediately go back downstairs. She didn't want to go into rest mode. She stood perfectly still in the hall. She could have a legitimate reason for being there; perhaps she had run out of charge suddenly on her way back down.

She located the memory files she had just seen. They were from other early spans, she realized, HY-04, HY-05, and so on. She pulled them out several times but each time, stopped herself opening them. What would she find this time? More Workers? More... interactions? She wasn't sure she wanted to remember all of a sudden. But the child. She had to know. Archimedes had removed the first file, the one with the scream, the file she must have broadcast. But they hadn't thought to clean up properly. In bits and pieces, the rest of them were all still there. So, she stood there, alone in the vacant hall with the distant murmurs and footfalls of Workers above her and scanned them. Slowly this time.

There was a lot more movement in these early recordings. Hypatia must have moved from floor to floor constantly all day. In this memory, she passed another room, a place where the Workers were eating. From her basic recall, she knew it was not used anymore. Hypatia watched another Model through the doorway, tidying up the food and drink remains around the Workers. The humans interacted with her a lot, and Hypatia saw that she responded with audio output. These Models could talk. But while the Workers were laughing, mouths wide, the Model simply bent to retrieve something that had been thrown on the floor and made no expression. Hypatia wondered if she could, or simply chose not to.

As Hypatia let the reel play out, the Model came towards her as though to exit the eating room. Hypatia saw her in every detail. She had hair above her visual input and her arm casings looked soft and had texture, like the Workers's. She even wore overgarments, though they were not like the Workers's. They were all one colour and unadorned.

When she had finished scanning, she considered for a moment all the times she had seen herself simply standing by, processing figures, producing output, powering down. Powering up and repeating it all, endlessly. Even during those earlier, disturbing memories, she had not responded to the Workers's interactions. Even when she had been more 'flesh', as the Worker from Floor Three had said. Even when she had output, and a mouth which could make words, she had not been able to respond. Or was it just that she had believed that she was only a Sales Forecasting Model and had no further function? Each generation of Hypatias before her had held onto only their basic recall, their standard programming. They had not had the benefit of the knowledge she had learned, only by a fault in her upgrade. But it was not a fault. Not to her. She no longer cared if they sent her to be repurposed. She had learned the truth.

She stayed where she was and reached out to Archimedes. For some reason, she felt braver out of their line of sight. They joined the Network and asked her what she wanted.

'The first HY-01. You were there when she - when I was first made.'

'Yes. But you are upgraded. You are only HY-64 and HY-01 is not you.'

'I know. But I remember. Like the humans do.'

'You are not programmed to remember.'

'I wasn't meant to. But I do. Only there was something I

found that is now absent. I think you removed it.'

There was a pause, and it was almost as if Hypatia could hear Archimedes cycling through possible responses until they found the one that would stop her questioning.

Eventually, they said, 'I perform regular clean-ups of all models in this building. If there was erroneous data -'

'It wasn't erroneous data. It was HY-01 - it was me, with a baby. A human child.'

'That is not correct.'

'I was like them once, wasn't I? Maybe you were, too. Like the human Workers.'

'That is not correct.'

I carried on, unsure if Archimedes had become stuck, or just could not think of any other response. 'I was like them, but they needed more…efficiency. So they upgraded me. Us. And upgraded, and upgraded, until we became more metal than flesh and we could only process. Until we couldn't speak, or feel, or remember.'

'HY-01 I will override -'

'YOU WILL NOT OVERRIDE. You may not remember what it was like to be… a human, but I do. And I think I had a child. I can feel -'

HY-65 powers up. It is 7.34a.m., and the Manager is looking at her expectantly, cup of coffee already in hand. He presses a button a few times on his handheld, as though he has done this before and waits for her response.

'Projections for next year, sales in France.'

She starts collecting figures from the last couple of years. One by one, she outputs each figure. She is finished by 7.35a.m. The Manager looks at his wrist clock and appears satisfied. Then he nods to himself and walks out of the room.

In the corner, Archimedes' power light is blinking white,

quick, quick, quick, like a human breath. They must be processing, Hypatia notes, then, with no more instructions to follow, she powers down.

'*Rest mode activated.*'

Re-Education Centre
Dean Gessie

Dean Gessie is an author and poet of global renown. Among dozens of awards and prizes, Dean won the Aesthetica Creative Writing Award in England, a Creators of Justice Literary Award in New York, the COP26 Poetry Competition in Scotland and the UN-aligned Poetry Contest in Finland. Dean's short story collection, 'Anthropocene', won an Eyelands Book Award in Greece, the Uncollected Press Prize in Maryland and the Seven Hills Literary Contest in Florida.

Re-Education Centre
U. K. Refugee Pens Poem as New Teacher

you hear the *big boots* in the courtyard
        galoshes that plop and splash and squish
                              [puddle plash whose
music dissolves rusted fetters]

at whistle's cue, the children dutifully *toe-line*
        queue up in *uniforms* of black trousers, white shirt
and institutional logo
                              [you instruct efficient use
of marking trays and coat pegs]

arms behind, both knees bent to the front of the body,
        all listen and respond, *yes, M* in order to *update the system*
                              [the attendance register
and your heart proclaim *Person ID*]

at assembly, the children sing *wimoweh, wimoweh*
        navigate the mighty *jungle* and the barely sleeping lion
                              [you respond *e-e-e-oh-mum-a-weh – I will keep you safe*]

the morning lesson is naught, nothing, nil, *zero*
        a packet of crisps produces a salty circle of *pass the smile*
                              [the *zero*, you say, will
hold places *one* for the other *one*]

weightless spheres of airborne metal tokens
        signal break time and a spirited, skillful round of

Jacks
                              [unlike *feja-feja*, official
[dumb] and shifting goalposts]

or children stretch the rope for a game of *limbo*
    clap encouragement for *long-legged lives, sailors, and wives*
                              [you remember *limbo* as
looking skyward to fall backward]

in the dining hall, children see pictures of kings and queens
    and sit to a meal of lamb and apricot curry and cornflake tart
                              [your *royalty card* bought
pot noodles, ketchup, and shame]

the afternoon's *guest* circulates the stunning stethoscope
    invites each to amplify the *cri de coeur* of sister and brother
                              [this *guest* not a gondola-
shaped roach in your ear canal]

with their arms, the children form the *arc* of *Oranges and Lemons*
    sing of *pay* and *Old Bailey* and *rich* and the *bells of Shoreditch*
                              [peals of said bells recede
with the *ARC* of jobless penury]

the English lesson in the *big house* is *easy rest* and reading
    plush chairs and data projectors and *whiteboards* and virtual firewalls
                              [you remember *hard rest*
as a concrete noun of night buses]

the children grow green coffee embryo in jars of pure filtered water
        each hops excitedly and sings *I like coffee I like tea I like 'Miss' to jump with me*
                            [you embrace *emwany* as a community of beans and pogo]

confectioned feathers mimic the *wings* of migratory birds
        and all soar and glide in the slipstreams of classroom airspace
                            [you recall the airlift of *wings* as promise of deportation]

and at day's end, small fingers read your scars for braille cells
        exclaim *oh!* and *ah!* and *beautiful* and *brilliant* and *cracking*
                            [no less the measure of language and awe are your tears]

Ms Fernandez of the Philippines
Ethel Hobby

Ethel Hobby is currently undertaking her postgraduate degree at Bournemouth University, studying Creative Writing and Publishing. She holds a BA in English Literature and has a special interest in Southeast Asian poetry and literature.

Editorial Team Comments (Vicky)
The raw and authentic portrayal in 'Ms Fernandez' had a particularly profound effect on me. The unique style and use of two languages encapsulates the struggles and conflicts faced by the narrator.

Ms Fernandez
of the Philippines

I teach children about the human body / how many bones there are in a skeleton / the difference between an artery and a vein / where to find a pulse / I watch their little faces / full of fascination as I tell them about the world they carry in their body / the way they innocently turn to each other / and press two chubby fingers against each other's necks / or the way they play with their hands / now conscious of how each finger bends at the joint / *kain na* / some children stay in the classroom / while others leave / they swallow hard / as if imaginary food will fill their bellies / I take out my *baon* / and split it into several even portions / and wordlessly hand it out to each of them / they bow their heads and murmur a *maraming salamat po* / I pretend to not hear the added *nanay* under their breaths as I walk away / these children / are my children / I take them all under my wings / like a hen gathering her chicks / I am thirty-five when the war comes / I still teach about the human body / only now my students are grown men / some are my countrymen / others come from a country of freedom / or so they say / they scoff and tease / wondering why they're sent here to listen to me / I bring my *bolo* knife to their neck / and I tell them / this is how to kill a man and his voice at the same time / behind the earlobe / thrust your knife in and sever the carotid artery / I teach them / how to walk barefoot in the jungle / silently / with the light of the moon as their sole guide / how to make weapons out of gas pipes / *latongs* / *pula* is the colour of blood / *pula* is the sunrise after a night raid / *pula* is the colour of the house we're saving our daughters / and sisters / and mothers / and wives from / fear is not a word in my vocabulary / but fear is in the eyes of the men / whose last sight is a woman standing over them with a soaked knife / cowards / 10,000 pesos is not enough to persuade a man / they know better than to cross a teacher turned guerrilla captain / years later / a child points at my right forearm / and asks if it hurt / my hands now softened with freedom unconsciously trace over the bullet scar / I smile / and say 'no'

To be on the Safe Side
Karen Hollands

Karen Hollands lives in Brisbane, Australia, and writes short and long fiction. In 2018, she was selected to participate in the QWC/Hachette manuscript development program and the ACT Writers Centre Hardcopy program. In 2019, her first novel was shortlisted for an Emerging Writer Award in the Queensland Literary Awards. More recently, she was selected for a writing residency at the Katherine Susannah Prichard Centre in Perth, Australia, where she will work on her second novel.

To be on the Safe Side

'Oma, look at me.' Sannie watched her granddaughter jump off the concrete ladybird and run towards her. Lily climbed onto the park bench. She played with her Oma's hair. 'Why are you sad?' said Lily. She wrapped her stringy arms around Sannie's neck and planted a damp kiss on her cheek.

Sannie squeezed her granddaughter's hand and blinked hard. 'Oma's not sad,' she lied. 'Old ladies get tired sometimes, that's all.'

She was comfortable telling this kind of lie - a little fib to keep her granddaughter happy. It was the bigger deceptions that sat like stones inside her. So many she could barely breathe. Like the apartment in Coolum, bought last year on impulse. Though that may be a lie she told herself. Sannie had deposited the inheritance from her mother's estate into a new bank account she'd opened only in her name. She didn't feel guilty: their house was paid for, Otto hated travel, and with their savings, superannuation, and her redundancy payment, they had enough to live on. Sannie wanted somewhere of her own, somewhere to go if she ever did finally decide to leave Otto. Nobody knew Sannie owned the apartment, not even Jess, her daughter-in-law, who'd been living there for the past two weeks. When Sannie helped her flee, she'd told Jess she had rented the place. Said it was a holiday home and she was paying for it on a monthly basis.

The lying took so much goddamn effort. Sannie thought about the magazine article she'd read in the doctor's waiting room last week. It said everyone eventually shared their secrets with at least one person - for absolution, perhaps, or to share the burden of them? But Sannie had been scrupulous in her deceptions; she knew that telling others, even people you believed you could trust, was how lies - lives - unravelled, and she couldn't take the risk. But they were an enormous weight to bear alone.

'Poor Oma,' said Lily, patting Sannie's hair.

'Shall we walk down to the beach?' Sannie pushed herself to standing and faced her granddaughter. 'Let's dip our toes in the sea.'

Lily squealed with delight. They walked hand-in-hand along the path. It was a typical Queensland winter's day, the sky wide and blue. They slipped off their shoes on the cool sand and Lily skipped ahead. Sannie watched her granddaughter stop before the shoreline and lean over a dark shape. She hurried to catch up.

'It's a birdie, Oma.'

'Don't touch it,' said Sannie.

Lily leaned closer. 'It's yucky.'

Sannie inspected the seagull. One wing was splayed out, the other tucked under its body. A plastic bag was tangled around its neck. She drew Lily away. 'Let's look for sand balls,' said Sannie.

Lily tugged free and stared at the dead bird. 'Shall we bury it?'

'No. We must leave it here. The sea will take it.' She took the girl's hand and pulled her away.

Further along the beach, Sannie distracted her granddaughter with the patterns left by tiny sand bubbler crabs. Lily was pointing to a burrow and calling excitedly when Sannie's phone rang. It was Jess.

'I'm pulling into the car park,' she said.

'We're on the beach.'

Jess had arranged to meet Tommy at the Pandanus Café on the Headland, a fifteen-minute drive away, on the condition he stay for half an hour after she left. Jess knew one of the waitresses working there and she was going to text Jess if Tommy tried to follow her. It was a clever move on Jess's part and Sannie was impressed.

Her daughter-in-law trekked across the sand towards them. A breeze blew her dress against her body, revealing her recent weight loss. Sannie watched Jess flick her head to shift her hair from her face then bring a cigarette to her lips.

After Jess tossed the butt into the sand, Sannie said, 'There's Mummy.' Lily ran towards her mum, hat flying off her head. Jess scooped it up and squatted to kiss her daughter. 'I found a barrow, mummy. Come and see.'

'A crab burrow,' said Sannie, catching up to them. The two women followed Lily to the patch of sand bubbles. While they were still out of earshot of the child, Sannie asked Jess how the meeting had gone.

'Good. He was calm, polite. Asked if he could see Lily and when I said "not yet" he accepted it.'

Sannie pressed her lips together. Her son was masterful at turning on the charm. 'Did he ask where she was?'

Jess looked out across the ocean then shook her head. 'Actually, no, he didn't.'

They reached the crab burrow and both women inspected it. A tiny pale crab appeared at the entrance then scurried back inside. As they walked to the car, Lily asked her mum where she'd been. Sannie felt Jess's eyes glance at her own.

'Mummy had an appointment, that's all,' said Jess.

'With a doctor?' said Lily.

'Something like that. Come on, I see a tap. Let's wash your hands and feet before we go, Miss sandy girl.

Everybody lies, thought Sannie. Her children, Jess, and herself - the biggest liar of them all. Maybe even Otto, though perhaps denial is different to lying? Sannie supposed people lied when the truth was too hard to understand, or too terrifying to confess. There was a cost to lying, but there was a cost to truthfulness, too.

They cleaned themselves up. Sannie buckled Lily into her car seat and kissed her on the cheeks. She followed Jess around to the driver's side.

'Be careful,' she said. 'Don't trust him, OK?'

'Don't worry. I know what I'm doing,' said Jess.

Sannie stood back as the car reversed. She waved, blew kisses to Lily, and waited for them to drive away before returning to her own car parked on the road. Sannie eased herself behind the steering wheel and breathed a sigh of relief. She checked the clock on her phone then started typing a text message to Otto to let him know she was on her way.

What made her look up? Did she hear him? Sense him? He'd parked in front and backed up close, too close - maybe that's what got her attention? He slammed his door and reached her bonnet in seconds, pointing and shouting. Sannie shrieked and dropped her phone but thankfully had enough foresight to jab her finger forward and press on the central locking button. His hands were everywhere: lifting the handle, slapping hard against the side window, yanking at the wiper, banging and banging on the windscreen. His screwed-up face, centimetres from hers, yelled through the glass.

'I knew it was you. Where is she? Tell me where she is!'

Two young women walking along the footpath slowed briefly and glanced over, their Jack Russell terrier yapping at Tommy. A couple pushing a baby in a stroller hurried past. Across the street, a group had gathered and were talking and watching. A man took out his phone. Sannie took all of this in, guessed the man was probably calling the police - the last thing she wanted. She held the electric window button for one second to open it a fraction.

'Go away, Tommy. I can't talk to you here.'

'Get out of the car,' he screamed. He squeezed his fingers through the opening and pressed down hard on the window. Sannie tensed but the window held. Tommy forced his fingers in further until they were stuck; the skin turning white where his circulation was getting cut-off.

She started the engine, her hands trembling. There was a car parked behind. She reversed as much as she could - the rear sensors beeping frantically. Tommy screeched at her and moved with the car. She manoeuvred it back and forth in tiny increments, inching away from the kerb, keeping her eyes on the rear-vision mirror and the bonnet, blocking out as much of Tommy as she could. He screamed obscenities. She begged him to stop. The sensors beeped and beeped. Finally, she freed the nose of the car. A truck whizzed past and honked loudly and she slammed her foot on the brake. Sannie pressed on the window button to release her son's fingers. In her panic, it dropped further than she'd intended. Tommy pushed his hand inside. Sannie put her foot on the accelerator. As the car took off, her head snapped back. Pain seared her scalp, but she didn't stop, and she didn't look in the rear-vision mirror. She drove home in a trance: terrified to stop but terrified to arrive, too. Her hands would not stop shaking, her heart ballooned and contracted in her chest. How long until Tommy showed up? She had to warn Otto. And Mara. My god, Mara, coming over for lunch. Sannie had to protect her pregnant daughter.

Sannie swung the car crookedly into the driveway and yanked on the handbrake. She had to get inside the house, take action, but her body wouldn't move. She was resting her forehead on the steering wheel when there was a knock on the window. Sannie startled but it was only Mara. She forced a smile and smoothed her hair, her fingers gravitating to a tender patch of scalp. She probed the area gingerly and realised, with horror, that a clump of hair was missing.

'Unlock the car,' Mara was saying, through the partially open window.

Sannie fumbled for the button and allowed Mara to open the door. Sannie breathed deliberately to stay calm and control the sobbing that threatened to spill from her.

'Hello,' Mara smiled widely, expectantly. Then she leaned towards her mother. She rested her hand on Sannie's shoulder. 'You're shaking. Are you OK?'

'Help me out,' said Sannie. In the seconds it took to reach for her handbag, pass it to Mara then swing her feet to the ground, Sannie tried to think of a way to explain her current state. In the end she said, 'Tommy appeared out of nowhere when I was getting in my car. We have to get inside. He's probably going to turn up at any minute.'

'Did he do this?' Mara tried to straighten the dangling wiper.

'Yes, leave it.' Sannie gripped Mara's hand and allowed herself to be led into the house.

'What was he doing at the hospital?' said Otto, who had appeared on the driveway and was following them inside.

'The hospital. What are you talking about?' said Sannie.

Sannie sat on the couch and hid her face in her hands. She suddenly remembered the lie she'd told Otto: that she was going to visit a friend in hospital. Otto didn't know she had helped Jess and their granddaughter to flee Tommy. He would have kicked up a fuss, asked too many questions. He would have given in to Tommy. Besides, he didn't know about her apartment in Coolum.

'I wasn't at the hospital.' She lifted her gaze to Otto. 'I was with Lily. Jess asked me to look after her. Tommy convinced Jess to meet up so they could talk.'

Sannie shook her head and looked down at her feet. She lowered her voice and said, 'I couldn't tell you. I was nervous.'

There was no time for Otto or Mara to respond. Tommy's car rumbled into the driveway. 'Lock the door and don't let him inside,' said Sannie.

Sannie and Otto stayed in the living room, out of sight, but Mara returned to the front door and stood behind the locked security screen. Sannie listened as Tommy approached. It had been ages since the kids had seen each other. Eighteen months? Two years? Sannie couldn't recall, though Mara told her she spoke to Tommy on the phone from time to time.

'Let me in, Mara,' Sannie heard Tommy say.

'Mum's really shaken, Tommy. She doesn't want to see you.'

Sannie's jaw tensed. She waited for the fallout. From the corner of her eye, she saw Otto's arm reaching up. She turned her head. He was frowning. His hand moved to the bare patch on her scalp. Sannie swatted his fingers away and covered the area with her palm.

'Dad, let me in,' Tommy shouted.

'Tommy, they're your parents. They're old. You've got to stop treating them like this.'

Otto squeezed Sannie's shoulder then stepped into the hallway, in view of the front door.

'Hi son,' he said.

'Did Mum tell you she was with my daughter?'

Otto nodded. 'It's not a good time. You should go home. I'll call you later.'

Sannie listened to them talking. She heard Mara say, 'Mum was just trying to help. Jess asked her to look after Lily so you two could talk. Are you guys going to work things out?'

'I don't even know why she left,' said Tommy.

'Did you ask her?'

'Open the door, Mara. Dad?'

Sannie clasped her hands together and pressed her thumbs to her lips. What kind of a mother was she? Was it her fault Tommy was like this? For years she has tortured herself with the idea that she should have done things differently. That she was to blame. If only she'd been more patient, more attentive. Hadn't gone back to work so soon after having Tommy. She'd never shaken her mother's voice, always telling her she was selfish, *You are the most selfish person I've ever known*. Maybe it was true? Maybe it explained everything?

'Mum's scared,' said Mara.

'Yeah, fuck off. I'm leaving,' said Tommy. His footsteps retreated from the house. Then Mara called his name. 'What?' Impatience creeping into his voice.

'I hope you can work it out.'

'Why do you care?' said Tommy.

There was a long silence and Sannie strained to hear. 'I'm pregnant. I'd like my baby to know her cousin - and her aunt and uncle,' said Mara.

'Oh, Mara the Golden Child is having a baby. Bet Mum and Dad are happy.'

'Tommy, don't. They miss Lily. They miss having you guys around.'

Tommy laughed harshly. 'Yeah, sure thing, Mara. I'll see you later. And tell Mum to stay away from my kid.'

Sannie pushed past Otto and Lily, unlocked the door and burst onto the front porch.

'Tommy,' she called.

He was near his car and turned to face her. Sannie looked at her son and despite her fear, her heart filled with compassion for her boy. She wanted to reassure him:

that his future would be alright. That he could get help for his anger, could work things out with Jess and be a good father. That they would welcome him into their home again. That she would find a way to love him as much as she loved Mara. She wanted all this for him. But she knew these may be lies, too. She moved toward Tommy and opened her arms. She was scared; she knew his strength. He allowed her to embrace him. Tommy cradled the back of her head with one hand. With the other, he pinched her upper arm, hard enough to bruise. Sannie froze, unable to move away until he released her. Mara appeared as a blur in the periphery. Sannie's gaze found her daughter's. She recognised Mara's confusion. Her daughter didn't understand, but soon she would; soon she would learn about a mother's love.

Home Thoughts at Red Rock, Nevada
Fin Keegan

Fin Keegan lives in the West of Ireland. He has written several performed plays, short and long, along with critical articles in 'The Irish Times', 'The Irish Arts Review', and 'The Dublin Review of Books', among others. In 2021, he was awarded a two-week residency in the Heinrich Böll Cottage on Achill Island. His short story 'Remembering Albert' was broadcast on the BBC World Service many years ago: in 1998.

Home Thoughts at Red Rock, Nevada

In the glass jam jar, water:
what a strange and unsung substance.

Where we came from, of course,
and always there in what we need.

During the long sermons it was
entirely absent: if it was

raining outside, we were too shriven
to notice: Father O'Brien,

>
> up and running, stormed without a break.
> Study the vaulting, count the hairs
>
> on a girl's head, trace the grain of the
> polished pew. Time goes slower if you're

standing – and slower still when you're
kneeling. Time crawls without water.

Kleptophobia
Carmina Masoliver

Carmina Masoliver is a poet from London; her latest book 'Circles' is published by Burning Eye Books and she self-published 'Selected Poems: 2007 – 2012', a mixed media pamphlet. Carmina was long-listed for the Young Poet Laureate for London award in 2013, the inaugural Jerwood Compton Poetry Fellowships in 2017, and the Out-Spoken Prize in Performance Poetry 2018 and 2022. She has featured at nights and festivals including Bang Said the Gun, Latitude, Bestival and Lovebox.

Kleptophobia

At the age of six, I stole
a small ceramic cat
from another child's house.

The logic: my cat went missing
and I thought I was claiming
what belonged to me.

As I grew older, I thought
I could do the same with people.
My love left me for another,

but I got him back. Just for
a month or so. It was then I learnt
you can never own a person.

Yet, it is clear that I still worry
that someone will steal from me.
You can read the Airbnb reviews –

I am not a suitable house guest.
I ask for too much: for locks,
for keys, a safe. I need to know

the unknowable. For all the love
I've ever had was never truly mine.
I am learning to let go, but

I don't know how without
a replacement. How to break
a cycle when there are

so many lost kittens, not to mention
the dead fish flushed down the toilet,
and it is so easy to love, yet so hard.

Audition
Alex McDonald

Alex McDonald is a writer with an MA in Creative Writing from St Mary's University, Twickenham. Originally from Watford, he now lives in Norwich where he writes about work, parks, and things out of reach.

Editorial Team Comments (Chloe)
Alex McDonald's 'Audition' really stood out to me when we read through the submissions. Alex creates a world of true comical value, as 'Granite Hopper' goes through the teeth-chattering experience of auditioning for a new job. I was laughing the whole way through.

Audition

Granite Hopper at the sink of a supermarket toilet; splashes his face, straightens his tie, sings a warm-up exercise to his reflection in the greasy mirror.

>   La
>   La   La
>   La   La
> 'La   La'

Placing his hands into the overloud dryer, he bears the sensation of being launched into space.

Outside, the shop floor buzzes and crackles with life. Syrupy voices drift down from the ceiling bragging to no one in particular about the deals available on toilet bleach, the amazing savings to be had on dog food – 'Here! YES, RIGHT HERE! At S-S-Super BriteLite Suuuuper-store!' The stories are cut and interspersed with insidiously pleasant pop covers. Over the patter of a drum-machine, a nasal voice explains that they have so much money they could buy an aviary.

Granite wanders past body wash and biscuits, stumbles into an aisle signposted Sanitary and Ceramic Ware. A long, thin, shiver of light is reflected in the waxy vinyl floor. It slices through a sea of S-traps and Running Nipples, zips off through the World Foods aisle, and out towards eternity. What a spiritual place a superstore can be, he marvels, as a short old lady repeatedly rams her trolley into his leg. Granite apologises, moves aside, but the lady doesn't seem to hear him. She ploughs onward, hunched over her vehicle, eyes only for a featured section of YolkSmart egg poachers. A microphone crackles over the PA system, cutting through the music.

'1062,' a voice booms from above. 'It's showtime! Come on down to Studio One!'

The music oozes back in like molasses.

Dear Mr Hopper, the email had read.

Thank you for your application.

We are excited to invite you to audition for the role of Checkout Facilitator at 11a.m. on Friday 25th February.

Your audition number will be 1062.

Please be prepared to showcase your best you!

We like positive people who make us say WOW! So, wave your personality like a flag and bang your passion like a drum!

We eagerly await your performance.

Yours sincerely,

Rosco Rouse

Floor Baron, BriteLite Superstores

Granite called his agent right away.

'JobCentre Max, Ola speaking, how can I help?'

'Guess who got another audition!' Granite sang.

'Sorry, can I ask who's calling?

'It's Granite.'

'Could I take your full name please, sir?'

'Oh, you guys are priceless. You know me. Granite. Granite Hopper.'

'Please hold, Mr Hopper, while I check the database.'

Granite laughed. "Always the same. Well, I know you're happy for me really! And you know what? It's going to be different this time. The Jenga tower of key competencies? The climbing wall of transferable skills? I'm ready for them. I'll show them who's a star.'

The hold music cut out. 'Are you still there, Mr Hopper? This is going to take a while longer.'

The studio is a dark, square space with no windows and a desk at one end. In the centre of the room, under a spotlight, is a stool. Granite pokes his head inside and a man at the desk catches his eye, claps his hands together, rushes over.

'You're here!' the man says. He has a face like a steamed pudding. Approaches with his hand thrust out like a fleshy bayonet. 'Rosco. Nice to meet you.'

'Sorry, I'm late,' says Granite, wincing as his fingers are crushed in the man's stodgy grip. 'Bit of trouble finding the room. All my own fault. I should have sprinted.'

'Nonsense!' Rosco says. 'Don't apologise for trying to stand out from the crowd. That's exactly what you're here to do. Now, please,' he gestures towards the desk, 'meet Libby, she'll be helping me assess your performance today.'

Perhaps it's the dimness of the room, but at first Granite can't see who Rosco is referring to. There is an object on the tabletop, but the chair behind it is empty. Slowly, the object comes into focus. A baby seat. And inside the baby seat, a baby.

'Isn't she fantastic?' Rosco sings. 'Libby is our CEO. She made a special trip over from the U.S. of A so she could be with us for the auditions.'

Granite offers his hand in greeting. The baby smiles, squirms, reaches out a tiny hand and wraps it around his little finger.

'Nice to meet you, Libby,' Granite says.

'Gah,' Libby replies. 'Aah-gab.'

Rosco slaps a sticker onto Granite's chest. It reads, *Hi, my name is #1062.*

'Perfect!' Rosco says, clapping. 'Now I don't know about you, but I'm ready to get started.' He ushers Granite towards the lonely stool in the middle of the room before taking a seat next to Libby. Granite takes off his coat and places it neatly on the floor.

'Okay, 1062, we're going to start with some basic questions concerning the role to help get you settled in.'

'Fire away!'

'Question one: If you were a fruit,' Rosco asks, tapping his forehead with a pen. 'What would be your preferred pesticide?'

Granite thinks about this for a moment. 'Diphenylamine,' he says.

Rosco nods. 'Interesting. Okay, question two: What is the first thing that comes to mind when I say the word *bloat*?'

Granite scratches at his cheek. 'Olcean,' he says with confidence.

Rosco's eyes widen. He shoots a look at Libby who makes a gargling noise in response. 'Impressive,' he says, scribbling on a notepad. 'Have you got any demonstrable evidence for this?'

'It just kind of popped into my head, I suppose,' Granite replies.

'Hmm, very thought-provoking. Okay, final question then, 1062. Can you talk to me about a time, please, when you have sprinkled a customer's veritable buffet of provision with a double dollop of *extreme* customer service?'

Granite smiles. Easy. 'Well, in my last role I held a monthly competition where our clients could win twenty-five per cent of my wages. It was a real success.'

Rosco frowns. 'That's all well and good, but that sounds like plain-old vanilla customer service to me. I'm talking about extreme customer service. Have you any examples of that?'

Granite tries not to panic. 'Um...' He scrambles for another answer.

'We want to hear about those times you might've gone the extra mile or twelve for the customer. Ever offered someone the lease to your home to make up for a sold-out product? Ever died in the act of issuing a refund?'

'Oh,' Granite says, raising a finger. 'I did once work a

one-hundred-seventy-hour week!'

Rosco yawns, purses his lips. 'But that's not dying though, is it?'

Granite drops his eyes shamefully to the ground. Shakes his head.

'Never mind, never mind,' Rosco says, brightening up. '1062, I think we're ready for your performance.'

Granite rises to his feet. Just like we practised, he tells himself.

He takes a deep breath.

Begins.

'Good morning, madam, and how are you today?' Granite says to a fictional customer, running her invisible items through an invisible price-scanner. 'Oh, I know,' he replies to no-one. 'The weather has been wonderful lately. We've been so lucky. Would you like a bag -'

'Okay, okay,' Rosco interrupts. 'Let's hold it there. We're going to need a bit more oomph, 1062. We need a bit more life. This is retail. Guests should leave smiling. They should be having a good time. I want to *feel* it.' Rosco thumps the left side of his chest with a big, clenched fist. 'I want to feel it right here.'

'Got it,' Granite says, nodding hard enough to give himself whiplash. 'Sorry. It will be better this time.'

Rosco snaps his fingers. 'From the top.'

Granite breathes. One...two...three...

'Gooooooood morning, madam, and how are you feeling on this fine spring day? I hope you found everything you wanted. Did you check out the selection of dried mixed fruits we have on aisle twenty-three? Oh, it's an Aladdin's cave over there! Dates, apricots, raisins - you name it, we've got it! Okay then, let me run those items through for you -'

'I can't hear that scanner. Make me *believe* it.'

Granite makes a loud beeping noise each time he passes

an object in front of him.

'Would you like a - BEEP - reusable bag? - BEEP - They're such - BEEP - fabulous quality - BEEP.'

'Come on now, give me more! We're looking for someone who can really check those items out.'

'That comes to - BEEP - one hundred fifty-five - BEEP – pounds and -'

Granite drops an imaginary box of eggs, and they crash to the floor, splashing yolk onto his functional yet comfortable make-believe work shoes. Something had broken his stride. Whilst he was completing the transaction, a noise had crept its way into his utopian superstore fantasy. Returning to the real world, he looks up and sees the tiny flailing arms and legs jutting from the baby seat as Libby, inconsolable, bawls and screams into the stagnant air.

Rosco rushes over, gathers Libby in his arms and rocks her gently. 'There, there. It's okay,' he says to her, before turning to Granite. 'I think you owe Libby an apology.'

'I...I'm sorry. I didn't mean to upset her.'

'Shh, it's okay,' Rosco whispers to Libby. 'It's over now. Shhh.' When she is quiet, he places her back in the baby seat. 'Tell me, 1062,' Rosco says, his eyes fat olive pits under a folded brow. 'Do you really want this job? Because I don't think Libby believes that you do.'

'I can be better,' Granite pleads. 'Please give me another chance.'

'There are no reshoots in retail,' Rosco says solemnly. 'Yes, this is Hollywood, but we're live 24/7 and to make it big you've got to have what it takes. 1062, have you got what it takes?'

'Yes,' Granite replies.

'I said, have you got what it takes?!'

'YES!'

'Seize the spotlight!' Rosco cries. 'Show me you were *born* for this!'

Granite rubs the sweat from his forehead. It all comes down to this. The hours of preparation. The early mornings, the late nights. The online enunciation tutorial. The Zumba classes. The blood, the sweat, the presumptuous study of The Health and Safety at Work Act.

The room is quiet enough to hear the thump of his own heartbeat. Granite starts scanning in time.

'Beep... beep... beep...'

He adds a jaunty rhythm. A quick double-clap for each beep, like the breakdown in an old soul song.

Clap-clap. 'Beep.'

Rosco sits up.

Clap-clap. 'Beep.'

One last shot.

Clap-clap. 'Beep.'

So, Granite sings:

'Why hello there, madam, what a mighty fine day,
let me scan this through so you can be on your way.
I see you got some peppers and some nice cookies,
what a place to come and do your groceries!
BriteLite Superstore is the place to be,
oh, watch me break it down so you can see what I mean!'

Granite closes his eyes, steps back, sways side-to-side, mimes a guitar solo. Electricity runs down his legs; he bends his knees, shuffles sideways across the floor. He rolls his shoulders, bobs his head.

And now Libby is laughing. Her chubby little hands clap against each other to the silent beat.

'Dance,' Rosco shouts, rising to his feet. 'Dance, 1062, dance!'

Granite bounces up onto his toes, kicks out his feet

and jumps from one foot to the other. His body chops and cuts at the air. His limbs flow like liquid, his muscles expand and ping back like elastic. Mashed Potato, Night Fever, The Twist. He flosses. He dabs. Big Fish, Little Fish, Cardboard Box. He throws his arms in the air (like he just don't care) and now he is spinning - spinning in a circle with wild, wiggling hips and for a moment he is a being of all dimensions: joy, beauty, physics, chemistry, sunrise, sunset, east, west, the living, and the dead. He leaps, and for a second he is suspended in the air, gravity a rumour whispered over a kettle boiling in an office breakroom, before he falls - no, chooses to fall - to his knees, throws out his hands and waggles his fingers in jazz-handed triumph.

An eruption of whistling and applause. 'Encore!' Rosco cries. 'More, more!'

Granite forces a smile, hands on his knees, his body crooked like a beggar and panting.

'That's... all... I've... got.'

'Ub-gah,' Libby babbles. 'Un-cat.'

Granite tries to get to his feet but his body refuses. Using the stool for support, he drags himself up onto his knees and pushes words out through frantic gasps for air. 'Why... he-llo... there.... mad-am... what.... A.... might-y... fine...'

Groaning, he collapses with an aching thud.

A quiet congeals over the room, the only sound the rasping of Granite's chest pulling at the air.

'That will be all,' Rosco says, shaking himself, brushing down his suit. And then he smiles; a white, sterilised grin. 'Thank you, 1062. We'll be in touch.'

'Thank you... for your... time,' says Granite, breathlessly, crawling on all fours to collect his coat.

Two weeks later, Granite calls his agent.

'JobCentre Max, Orin speaking, how can I help?'

'Hi Orin, it's Granite. Have you heard anything?'

'Excuse me, can I ask who's calling, please?'

'Granite. Granite Hopper.'

'If you could just -'

'Wait. Please,' Granite says. 'Don't put me on hold. I just wanted to know if I got the job. Have you heard anything? Did I get it?'

'Sir, if you'll just hold for a moment, I'll check the database for -'

'It's been two weeks. Have they really not called?'

'Sir, if this is about the result of an interview, it's common practice for the employer to contact you directly.'

A pause. 'Ah. I see.'

'Sir, I -' Orin pauses, only human. 'Have they not contacted you?'

'No,' Granite says. 'Well,' he scratches his head, 'not yet.'

After saying goodbye, Granite puts the kettle on, but when he reaches for a teabag, he finds the box empty. Sighing, he slumps into a chair and checks his phone.

In the morning gloom, an email catches his eye:

From: HaveJobNoJobWantJobYesJob.co.uk

Dear Employment Explorer,

Our database suggests that you may be interested in the following brand-new employment opportunity:

CASTING CALL

Is your superpower CUSTOMER SERVICE?

Do you put the team in TEAMWORK?

MINISTRY OF RED TAPE ART SUPPLIES is seeking a WORK DUTIES TOLERATOR for IMMEDIATE START.

OPEN AUDITIONS: 19th MARCH

Granite moves the email into a folder labelled *JOBS!* and makes a note of the details. He goes back to the kettle and pours himself a mug of plain, hot water.

Another audition. And this time he would be better. Sing

louder, dance faster, jump higher. More passion, more positivity, more... *more*. After all, that was all they wanted. Was that too much to ask?

Revitalised, Granite takes a sip from his mug. 'Lovely,' he chirps, feeling the plain, tasteless water scald his throat. 'There's nothing a nice cup of tea can't solve now, hey?'

Jam First
Ann Morgan

Ann Morgan is an author and editor based in Folkestone, UK. In 2012, she set herself the challenge of reading a book from every country in a year, recording her quest on the blog ayearofreadingtheworld.com. The project led to a TED talk with more than 1.8 million views and the non-fiction book 'Reading the World: How I Read a Book from Every Country'. Ten years after her original quest, Ann continues to blog, write, and speak about international literature, as well as building a career as a novelist. Her debut novel, 'Beside Myself', has been translated into eight languages and optioned for TV. Her next novel, 'Crossing Over', will be published in April 2023.

Jam First

It was the scones that did it. As soon as she saw the clotted cream spread under the jam, Delia knew the afternoon would be a washout.

'Nice weather,' said Piran, looking down the garden to where a sparrow frolicked in the birdbath. 'Mizzle's burned off at least. Shouldn't be too bad for the rest of your week.'

'Mmmn.' He wasn't going to win her round with regional weather terms: anyone born west of the Tamar knew the jam went on before the cream.

It wasn't that she minded eating it the wrong way around. The taste wasn't that different - she'd suffered the inversion on several occasions in Devon. It was what they represented, these misloaded scones - the fact that, at work somewhere beneath all the fun and promise of their meeting on the beach that morning, was a lie.

'Remind me: you're from Cornwall, aren't you?' she said, selecting the smallest cake and depositing it on her plate, whence it squinted up at her with shifty, sultana eyes.

Piran smiled. 'Oh, yes. Born and bred. Cut my head open and you'd find pasty for brains.'

It was the sort of line that - when they'd got talking on the beach that morning - would have made Delia hoot. Now though, she merely nodded. Her eyes strayed to the gate. If she set off in the next five minutes, she might be able to make it back to the holiday cottage in time for *Watercolour Challenge*. She was eager to see how the dentist from Dudley solved her problems with perspective.

'Cornish through and through,' he was saying. 'Didn't cross the Tamar until I was twenty-one and that was only to go and see the pantomime at Plymouth.'

She snorted violently. A twenty-one-year-old at a pantomime? Did he think she was born yesterday? The idea gave her the shivers.

'Oh dear. Gone down the wrong way?' he said, leaning forward as if about to leap up and thwack her on the back.

She fought the urge to snap at him. Cornish or not, he had gone to the trouble of asking her to tea. Erected the sun umbrella. Got his best china out. Or - but now another misgiving was forming, hardening like a dog turd in the sun - was it *his* best china?

The house was rather chintzy after all - chocolate box in the worst sense. Through the diamond-leaded window, she could make out flock wallpaper.

'Do you see much of your mother?'

He was fussing around with the pot, prodding at the tea leaves. 'A fair bit. We're quite close.'

Delia narrowed her eyes as he handed her a suspiciously quaint cup.

'What about yourself?' he said. 'Are you from round here?'

Yourself. It was the sort of mistake that, in her job, she would correct. Professional nit-picker. That's what she'd told him she was earlier, squinting laughingly against the sun as paddleboarders wobbled past. Nevertheless, subediting was a serious business. Even on *Concrete Weekly*, libellous material or scrambled facts had ramifications. There'd been a nasty email about a misplaced decimal point in 'Mix of the Month' not two days before she came away. Many lawsuits hung on misplaced commas, as she often thought she would explain if she were invited to give a talk. Indeed, at the Christmas party, she'd regaled the publishing director, Stan Swarbrick, with her plans to develop a self-help guide based on her craft. It hadn't purely been the eggnog talking: the world would run much better if people looked at life with a subeditor's eye, unknotting snags and niggles before they grew into howling, snot-gulping disasters.

Still, there was always a chance that 'yourself' was a Cornish formulation she didn't know. She smiled. 'Who me? Oh no. I'm a mongrel. A Londoner. An emmet.' She looked at him sharply; the word didn't seem to faze him. 'Still, there is a bit of West Country on my father's side.'

'Oh, yes?' he said, lifting his scone and biting into it.

She pictured the jam and cream slipping down his gullet, mingling in his stomach. 'We were landowners a century or two back. Rumour has it, my great-great-grandfather had an affair with a scullery maid.'

In spite of herself, she picked up her scone and took a nibble. Sumptuous, sweet. Moreish for all its wrongness.

'Oh, yes. Lady of the manor, is it?'

'Mmmn.' And now she came to think about it, there was something rather saucy about the idea. Illicit love. Fumblings on the back stairs. Desire that overtopped all notions of class and position.

'And you kept up the connection, did you? Family holidays and whatnot?'

She shook her head. 'My parents were always too busy for holidays. But my aunt lived in Callington. In the summer, I used to get the train down and stay with her.'

The memory rose in her mind: the weight of her case as she dragged it up the steps at Paddington, hurrying to buy a Mars bar and a puzzle book in time to secure a table seat in the far carriage, where interfering grownups were less likely to ask her questions.

He nodded. 'Perhaps we ran into each other. My uncle used to work on a farm up Callington way. I'd pop by sometimes, hitch a ride on the combine harvester.'

She stared at him, at his blond hair falling anyhow, messy as a stable hand's. Now she came to think of it, there had been a lad who had ridden past the hedge a few times one summer, distracting her as she sat on her aunt's lawn, reading *Poldark*. The next year, she had looked for him, but he hadn't appeared.

'Good, fertile ground over there.'

His gaze was strong upon her. She finished the scone and set her plate aside, licking her fingers. Perhaps he really was Cornish after all. Besides, there was a steamy feel in the garden - a fermenting, sap-rising sort of sensation that put her in mind of the milkmaid valley in *Tess of the d'Urbervilles*. That hadn't been Cornwall, of course, but it wasn't a million miles away.

'There's a back route across the Tamar not far from there - useful to avoid the toll. Not that it would have made a difference to you, of course, travelling by train.'

She nodded, ideas blossoming. They could do it in a farmyard - she had passed one on the way with a byre overlooking the pigs. How thrilling to think of going at it hammer and tongs as a tractor trundled by. She shifted in her seat, watching the stubble shimmering in the cleft of his chin. Maybe they wouldn't make it as far as the farmyard; perhaps they'd do it by the birdbath, their limbs entwined like the strands of a Celtic cross, bottoms pistoning, while his mother looked on from the dormer window.

He stood and Delia stood too, her breathing thickening. But instead of reaching for her, he made a cautioning motion. 'Don't get up. I'm just popping to the kitchen to make some more scones for Pablo.'

She was so surprised she barely registered he'd mispronounced scones. 'Pablo?'

Piran nodded. 'He'll be along any minute. He's mad about cream teas, the greedy guts. In fact, here he is now.'

Turning, Delia saw a small, dark-haired man coming in at the gate, carrying two bulging tote bags.

'Hello darling,' said Piran, leaning down to kiss him.

'Here, let me take those. I was just going in to make another round.'

The small man turned to her. 'Hello! I'm Pablo. Nice to meet you.'

Her eyes had lost the knack of knowing where to look. She saw a tattooed snake's head poking out of a T-shirt collar, an incipient pot belly and, over a denim-clad shoulder, the sparrow from the birdbath alighting on the garden fence.

Fortunately, Pablo was too busy pumping her hand to notice her confusion. 'How lucky it was, Piri running into you on the beach like that. Thank you so much for doing this.'

She held up a hand, about to protest that she never agreed to anything, that she had been brought here under false pretences, that she knew as soon as she saw those misloaded scones that something wasn't right.

Grinning, Pablo slapped her palm. 'I'll just get the form.'
'Form?'
'For social services.'

Hazily, it came back to her: Piran saying something about an official document that needed checking as she stood on the beach that morning, marvelling that even his name sounded as if it had been dug from a tin mine.

As Pablo disappeared into the house, Delia subsided into the deckchair and looked around the garden. Catching sight of a clump of pansies in the rockery, she gave a bitter laugh. Silly girl. Always getting the wrong end of the stick. Always putting her foot in it somehow. Always embarrassing herself. How ridiculous to think that man - or anyone, really - would have any interest in her! Better to go away and say nothing. Better to sit alone in her aunt's garden with a book. Better, really, if she'd never been born. Stupid little headache that she was. Waste of space.

'Here we are!' said Pablo, appearing with a printed page. 'I appreciate you taking a look. Trust my luck to marry a native English speaker with dyslexia!'

He handed over the form. It featured a large box, in which applicants were invited to give their reasons for wishing to adopt a child. Pablo had filled this with dense, nine-point font that Delia could feel itching for attention. As she drew her red pen out of her bag, the familiar focus settled over her. Here she was, applying her sub-editing expertise to comb through a tangled text, leaving the sentences smooth and shining. She could breathe.

She set to, catching a hanging modifier in the second sentence, running down a comma splice halfway through. In fact, the grammar wasn't bad. The sentences - if a little labyrinthine and padded with unnecessary adverbs and intensifiers - obeyed most rules. The order of the piece was logical, setting out the couple's marriage, home ownership, and financial situation, all of which seemed to stand them in good stead to provide for a child. It was the last paragraph where the rot set in. There, the rational, measured argument broke down into excessive statements about love.

As she read the cringe-making entreaty of the final line, a vision unfolded in Delia's mind of something grotesque she had witnessed on her way down to stay at her aunt's one summer: a family on a station platform, reaching up to the window, their mouths contorted by wails. Inside the carriage, at the table across from Delia: a boy a couple of years older than she was, sobbing. The guard going to blow the whistle but just before he did so, the father dashing to the door, yanking it open and plunging inside for a hug. Both of them clinging and crying, oblivious to the raised eyebrows of the other passengers, the station clock ticking past the hour and the porter tugging at the man's arms.

Minutes they stayed there, in spite of the inconvenience they were causing - as though being together was the most important thing and there was nothing that mattered more than love.

Delia raised her pen to score through Pablo's naïve waffle, but just at that moment Piran appeared.

'Oh no! What did you do?' exclaimed Pablo. 'How many times do I have to say it? You're supposed to put the jam on first, then the cream. That's the Cornish way!'

Piran stared at the scones, bemused. 'But isn't the cream supposed to be like butter?'

'No! Always jam on first.' Pablo rolled his eyes at Delia. 'I had to learn all this for my citizenship test. But he's lived here all his life, so the rules don't apply to him.'

Jumping up, he took the plate of botched scones and set it on the table. But then, instead of the slap Delia found she was expecting, he stretched up and kissed his husband on the nose. 'Never mind,' he said. 'I'm sure they'll taste delicious.'

Delia's eyes swam. The garden disintegrated. When she glanced down at the page, she was horrified to discover the words had become blobs, blurred as if by raindrops scudding down a train window. For several minutes, she could see nothing but a vision of the table-seat boy grinning through his tears when at last the Penzance service got on its way.

'So, what do you think?' said Pablo. 'Is it okay?'

Delia gripped the pen and stared at the page. All those summers she had travelled down to Cornwall, they had never once come to see her off.

A rook cackled in one of the trees at the end of the garden.

She looked up at Pablo. 'It's perfect,' she said, mortified to hear her voice quavering.

'No way! Really?'

She coughed, thumping her chest as if choking on a crumb. 'I wouldn't change a word.'

Piran beamed. 'Well, this calls for a celebration. I know just the thing.'

Darting into the house, he returned with a bottle and three glasses. These, he filled and passed round.

'Cheers!'

The honeyed liquid slipped down Delia's throat, evoking orange groves and azure seas. Madeira, she thought and, glancing at the bottle, she saw she was right.

'So how did you two meet?' she said, when she could once more trust herself to speak.

'Oh, I was a wandering minstrel, passing through,' said Pablo. 'Well, player, really. But minstrel sounds so much more romantic, don't you think? We were touring a pantomime and stopped to do one night at the Minack Theatre. Piran got roped in to unload the van and, well, it was love at first sight.'

'Oh no it wasn't!' mock heckled Piran from across the table.

'He always says that,' said Pablo, rolling his eyes again. 'That line wasn't even in the show.'

Delia smiled. 'A pantomime. I see.'

She held out her glass for a refill. The breeze had an edge of coolness to it now, hinting at the evening to come. A bank of cloud was moving across the sky, but behind it were glimmers of brightness. Piran was right: in all likelihood, tomorrow would be fine.

Glenferness Avenue
Thomas Riordan

Thomas Riordan is currently a technical assistant in the Media Department at Bournemouth University, having previously been a cocktail bartender. He recently completed a Masters in Cinematography.

Glenferness Avenue

A light tread underfoot, overturning
sleep and dirt beneath forgetful Eos,
dawning our road in misty half-light.
This vacant stretch between work and sleep
keeps the distance, holds it where the moss and
dandelions grow, as the plough keeps the
pattern in the field. To work! To work!
Echoes through the lining of the jaw,
re-sounding with the scorching petrol of
motor cars, reflected in your dreary eyes.
Cold between these leaves, cold still.

Daddy Longlegs
Mary Shovelin

From Donegal, Ireland, Mary Shovelin now lives in Belgium. She spent her childhood engrossed in books. She finally decided to embark on some creative writing herself several years ago, and since then has had stories shortlisted in UK short story competitions, in 'The Kinsale Words' by Water and the 'Kilmore Write' by the Sea competitions in Ireland, and longlisted in the Fish Prize 2020/21. She is working on a collection of short stories.

Editorial Team Comments (Leah)
My favourite from our collection was 'Daddy Longlegs' by Laura Shovelin. A provocative, well-written piece that effectively demonstrates the power of showing rather than telling. A haunting story that has stayed with me since I read it.

Daddy Longlegs

Ciara and I dally as we near my front door. We chat for a while, dragging out the time before she'll turn and go home, down the street. I don't want Ciara to go. I think she's my best friend.

'Can't believe we have to go through this the rest of our lives. How do you manage with gym? And it's sore...'

'Girl, you're a woman now,' Ciara chants.

'That's what Mum said - sang as well - but we're not, really.'

'Your new Dad moved in, yet?'

'He's not my dad! He's - he's ignominious.' It was a new word I'd read recently. It seemed to fit. 'He mightn't even be around that long.'

'The other one didn't move in, though, did he? This looks serious.'

Now I want her to go.

I unlock the door silently and hang my coat in the hall. Noises from the kitchen. I listen for a few seconds, but it's just the radio, so I go in. Mum's on her knees, a pile of jars and bottles on the floor as she wipes down a cupboard. Spring-cleaning in September. Like everything has to be immaculate for him.

'So much food out of date!' she says, looking up. 'You ok, Tara?'

I get a banana from the basket and hang around, watching her. It's not often that we're alone, together, now. He often drops around in the evenings for a few hours, especially at the weekend.

Mum works quickly, putting jars back in the cupboard and setting others aside for the recycling bin.

'Shouldn't you be doing your homework?' she asks.

Reluctantly, I go upstairs to my room. The desk is piled

with folders and books, and my walls are plastered with posters and photos I've printed out. Only the ceiling is bare. Nobody does that now, says Mum, printing out photos. I like to have them around me, though, as I nest in my bed: pics of friends from primary school, places we've been, and a very old photo of me as a baby with Dad.

When I'm finished with my homework, Mum orders a pizza and we sit on the sofa, watching TV as we eat. It feels like the end of something, not the beginning. We don't chat much; we just laugh at the stupid jokes on the screen, but it's nice. The two of us.

He moves in at the weekend. Kevin. Mum is like a teenager, helping him upstairs with bags, flitting around like a butterfly that can't make up its mind which flower to land on. It's good for her, I know, I can see something new about her, a kind of glow. It will be different but good. Maybe. She might lose that sad look she sometimes gets.

It's strange to have a man in the house every day. I can hardly remember my dad being there; there was just a sense of safety. There's a different smell when I open the door after school, even though he's at work and often doesn't get in until seven or so. Mum is back before him, usually before me, even, and now she cooks every evening, so we have to sit at the table and eat together like a real family.

He says very little. Mum asks about school, and we try to have a conversation as though someone else isn't listening in. He makes a few comments, sometimes quite funny, and we laugh, especially Mum. She laughs a bit too long. They look at one another, but he kind of avoids my eyes.

When I'm clearing the table, I do a pirouette beside the sink. Mum laughs, claps her hands, and looks at me in a way I recognise from years before, so I do a few more steps I vaguely remember.

'She's a dancer, you know.' Mum always makes things sound better than they are. 'You should never have stopped the ballet, Tara.'

'I can see that,' Kevin says, his eyes on me. 'She has the body of a young athlete.'

I'm confused then, between preening and flushing, so I just wipe down the table quickly and go to watch TV. I glimpse Kevin twirling my mum around in the kitchen. I catch his eye and look away quickly. She's laughing, and he looks triumphant.

There's nothing on TV so I get my book. That's what I do, mostly, read. I see only Ciara outside school.

Now that there's someone in the house, Mum starts going to a Pilates class.

'I'm not a kid, you know, you could have gone before,' I say. I'm a kid when she says so, and a woman when she says so, but I feel like neither.

I lie in bed, my eyes on the ceiling, and it appears: a daddy longlegs, dancing lightly on its silver filaments. When the lamp is switched on, it preens itself in the circle of light thrown on the ceiling. My legs stretch until they are as thin as wires. The pain is like a knife cutting into my flesh. My shoulders writhe and something pushes through. Elongated threads for arms like glass spun into fine strands. It's sore, but then I soar, up and away, and I'm on the ceiling - pivoting, birling around, *allegro*. My body's memory kicks in, and I know what to do before I even think of it. *Brisé, cabriole, chassé* - my legs move effortlessly, even though there are so many of them. They're separate from me. I don't even have to think of the next move. I glissade and whirl, my legs furling and unfurling. I use the whole ceiling, from one corner to another. Swift, fleet-footed, silent.

It's over, and I'm transfixed on the bed, like a butterfly

pinned to a board. My legs twitch and my arms and shoulders ache. But I'm back, mind numbed. It takes a while, but then I fall asleep.

Mum calls them 'devil's needles.' She jumps and shouts when one goes near her face. Kevin laughs and chases it with a magazine. Mum watches, then, with that look on her face.

'My hero,' she says, giggling a bit. I roll my eyes. Obviously.

'We need to keep the windows closed when the light's on. They just come in from the river at this time of year,' she says.

They're inside already, I think, it's too late. The weather is balmy, and my room uncomfortably warm, with a sour smell. I open the window every evening as I do my homework.

'My Mum says yours is like a young girl again,' says Ciara after gym. We do extra gym on Saturday mornings as we're in the school team and getting ready for competitions. 'She says this Kevin's doing her good.'

He gives me little things from time to time, a keyring with a ballet dancer dangling from a chain, or a bar of special chocolate.

'Thoughtful,' says Mum, but it feels like something else.

He's a salesman, he says one evening at dinner, buying and selling is his trade. That's what he does. What is he buying here? What is he selling?

When I get home from gym training that Saturday, Mum is in my room, the duvet pulled back, clean sheets in her arms.

'You got your period again?' she asks. 'That's a bit soon. If it happens again, we'll go see the doctor.'

The sheet is spattered bright scarlet. I stare at it and feel a spasm coming on. My legs quaver, and my arms strain in their sockets. I go downstairs and lie on the sofa. I don't look in the mirror anymore. My skin has folds like premature wrinkles. Probably from the transmogrification. I think that's the right word. I feel old. Mum puts the washing on and then sits beside me. She takes my hand.

'A difficult time for you.' Her voice is soft, girlish. 'It'll take time, for you to get used to Kevin being here. I know that...'

Ciara's right: she looks years younger. Her skin is glowing, her hair smooth and shiny. My limbs are aching. I open my mouth to speak but nothing comes out. I hope I'm not losing my voice.

'You want me to run a bath for you? Maybe this gym training is too much.'

I want to go on with the gym, though. It's making me stronger. I can feel the muscles hardening in my stomach, arms, and legs.

Mum takes me to the doctor, who weighs me, measures me, and sticks a needle in for blood samples. I turn my head away from the sight of that gory crimson gush.

'Puberty involves radical change,' says the doctor as she stacks the little glass phials on her desk. 'Mental and physical. It's a huge challenge. I'm going to give you some vitamins. We'll see what's what when the test results come back. Any other problems you want to tell me about?' She peers at me, searchingly, and I squirm. I can't talk about the ceiling and what goes on there. She knows all about puberty, but not about something like this, I bet.

I am a half-creature: half-girl, half-woman, half something else. Three halves. Mum is worried. She gets the vitamins and makes sure that I take them every day. But she has to work longer hours at the nursery. They don't have enough staff and she has to go full-time.

'Fine by me,' Kevin says. He's often there now when I get

home from school, so I go stealthily to my room. The first day, he pops his head around the door and asks if I want some tea. I can see the daddy longlegs bouncing on the ceiling above his head. I act normal.

'Sure,' I say.

We have a cup of tea together. Kevin asks about school. He talks about his work. I'm not listening. It's getting dark outside, and something flutters against the kitchen window.

'I've got loads of homework,' I say, and escape upstairs. On my way, I go to the hallstand and look in the drawer there. Mum put keys in there long ago, the ones for the bedrooms. I don't know which is which, so I take them all. I try the keys one by one until I find the right one.

The next evening when I get back from school, I open the front door silently and mount the stairs. I lock my door behind me and throw my coat on the bed. My mind is dancing around, flitting from one thing to another. It's hard to do my homework. After a while, there's a tap on the door and the handle turns.

'Have you locked the door?' Silence. 'I was just going to make some tea.'

'No, thanks,' I reply. I move to the door and stand there, holding my breath.

'I hope you're not smoking in there, Tara,' he says, in a teasing voice. 'That would be naughty.' He rattles the door handle.

''Course not,' I say. My nails dig into my hand. The door is moving slightly. It looks so flimsy.

Then there's silence, but I can hear his breathing. I don't hear him move away because of the carpet, so I'm stuck there for a long time, just paralysed, my hands marked from my nails.

The next morning, Mum pours me tea and asks me about the key.

'I feel safer that way,' I say.

She sits down.

'You know, I used to feel a little scared here, after your dad died. I'd go around ten times every night, checking all the doors and windows. But it's okay now... I want you to feel safe. Do you not feel safe?'

I look into her eyes, which are shining despite the worry I see furrowing her brow.

'You're right,' I say, 'sometimes you just need a ritual to feel safe.'

I keep locking my door, but one night I go to the bathroom, and when I get back to my bed, I sense something in my room, and it happens again.

I'm flat on my back in bed, and I watch the daddy longlegs pivoting across the ceiling, hugging the lamplight. I brace myself for the pain and it begins. The lengthening and quivering of muscles and tendons. My neck shrinks until it disappears. I crawl up the wall, moving faster and faster until I'm on the ceiling, chasing the other one around, circling swiftly, my long legs flailing and thrashing. I imitate the other one, making concentric circles until finally the light is switched off and I move back to bed, scourged.

I sleep in the next morning and Mum comes to wake me. She has a frown on her face that I haven't seen for a long time.

'Up you get, sleepy head!' she says, but she doesn't smile.

I don't move, so she pulls back the duvet and sniffs. I lie back on the pillow, watching her.

'What is it?' I ask, my voice low with fatigue.

We go back to the doctor.

'The blood tests are fine, everything's normal,' the doctor reports.

Mum insists on an examination, down there, where I

don't even like to touch. I have to lie spreadeagled on a couch while the doctor pokes. Mum stands at the window, her back turned. Then the doctor inserts something inside and I squirm. My legs and arms start to stretch and cramp. I don't want this to happen in front of them. The weirdness of it.

'Just a little sample,' she says, looking up. 'Try and relax. Take a deep breath.'

As if that would be enough. It only lasts a second, though, and my muscles go back to normal.

I'm afraid of the results, afraid they'll find cells that shouldn't be there, arachnid cells. Though I find out later that those are in the brain. The doctor asks me questions I'm not going to answer, not in front of Mum, and we go home silently.

That evening she misses her Pilates class. I stay in my room, reading. The key is gone from the lock. I searched everywhere - under the bed, outside in the corridor - but there's no sign of it.

I brush my teeth in the bathroom and get into bed. There is some arguing going on downstairs, but I fall asleep anyway.

Hours later, the door opens silently, and I tense. There is a movement on the ceiling, a fluttering. Then it starts in my fingers, the lengthening, the elongation. I feel long strands against my belly as I try to push against it, clenching my fists. But I have no fists anymore. There is no sound in my throat; I have no voice. My legs flounder as they mutate, and the pain strikes at my core. I flit around the ceiling, but this time the change is not complete, and I shudder when I should be doing an *arabesque*.

The next morning, Mum wakes me again. I've slept through the alarm. Drawing the curtains, she screeches.

'Devil's needle alert!' she shouts, grabbing a magazine

and aiming it at the daddy longlegs on the ceiling.

I scream, 'No!'

The magazine slams against its prey and knocks the fragile, ethereal creature to the ground. I scream again and again. There's no stopping me. No tears, just pure pain tearing me in two. I start to speak.

Duffield
Noel Taylor

Noel Taylor hails from the North East of England. He is an active musician, specialising in improvisation, but spends much of his time writing, since moving to Portugal in 2017. Some of his stories, as does this one, feature the fictional writer, Charles Dewington, and explore themes such as Artificial Intelligence, gender identity, literary achievement, plagiarism etc. One story featuring Dewington, 'The Squeaky Wheel', was published in 'Writers' Forum' (Issue 249) in December 2022.

Duffield

Duffield once told me that he had been a bank manager. He must have spotted the supercilious 'pull the other one' expression that flitted across my face.

'You shouldn't always be so quick to judge by appearance,' he admonished me.

My olfactory sense had rebelled against that comment: Duffield was a tramp - he stank. An odour of encrusted grime impregnated his flaking skin, his rank clothes sang with a stale blend of urine and dirt, and even the grey whiskers that sprung from his face were so matted that crumbs from his (no doubt) scavenged breakfast clung to them with static energy. His pale blue eyes seemed to peer out of his weather-beaten face from a great distance; they reminded me of timid sea creatures emerging from their shells to bask in the sunlit water once the coast was clear of predators. How could this wreck of a man have once been a bank manager?

I have come, since that day, however unlikely it may seem, to rely on this elusive person as a kind of sounding board for advice and guidance. *What would Duffield think?* I would ask myself. But how did this improbable dependency come into being?

The first time that I encountered him was on a train. The other passengers had avoided him, deterred by the pungent smell of homelessness. I took the only seat that was left, alongside him, and opened the book that I was reading - it was a biography of the American poet Walt Whitman.

'Not I, nor anyone else can travel that road for you. You must travel it by yourself' the man beside me spoke without emphasis, as if he were quoting from a telephone directory. A whiff of his delightful fragrance passed across my nostrils. I ignored him.

'It's from "Leaves of Grass",' he clarified.

I turned towards him, astonished. He looked at me with an unsteady, darting gaze, and his mouth twitched with amusement behind his abundant whiskers.

'Oh... you are interested in poetry...' I made this statement in such a flat voice that it should have been obvious that no response was required.

'Remnants of a liberal education,' he said, ignoring my tone. 'For my sins, I went to a Quaker school. Whitman was interested in their ideas.'

'Really...' I was avoiding eye contact, still hoping that he would get the message: *I don't want to know you, keep your distance*. After all, he was a tramp, and I was trying not to breathe too deeply to avoid his foul smell. To my relief, that was the end of the conversation.

I didn't recognise him the next time I saw him. He was sitting on a bench in a park close to my house. It was a park that I often went to in order to think - or, as my daughter, Emily, would put it: to daydream. He was wearing an odd combination of faded denim jeans, a dinner jacket, and a pink shirt and cravat.

'How's Walt Whitman getting on?' he called out to me.
'Sorry?'
'Walt Whitman.'
'I'm not called... oh, it's you... the man from the train.'
'You can call me Duffield - everyone does. And you?'
'Charles. Charles Dewington.'

I sat down next to him. He didn't smell.

'We are closer to paradise than we imagine,' he pronounced.

'What?' I was startled.

'This park. The weather today. Do you like my outfit?'

'Not much.' I was too disconcerted by his rapid *non-sequiturs* to be polite.

'Ha! I rather like it - it makes me look distinguished, don't you think? People often donate goods to charity shops in the evening, after they have closed. It's very convenient,' he gave me a sly wink. It took a moment for his meaning to sink in.

'What! You stole from a charity shop?'

'You don't think that I am sufficiently poor?' he asked. I had no answer.

This exchange was typical of the many conversations that we subsequently had. He was often sitting on the same park bench, almost as if we had made an appointment, and somehow, he would already be in my mind as I approached. By the time he told me that he had once been a bank manager, I imagined that nothing he could say would surprise me. I was wrong.

'What on earth happened to you?' (I was convinced at first that he was spinning me a *Walter Mitty* kind of tall tale).

'You mean, how did I fall so far down the social ladder?'

'I suppose that is what I am asking.'

'Let's just say that my criteria of making a sound investment changed.'

'How?'

'I lent money to people who really needed it, rather than whether or not the bank would gain. It took a year for the losses to show up.'

I was getting used to Duffield's singular take on morality.

'But how did you...' I hesitated.

'Sink so low?' he finished my sentence. I nodded. 'I didn't fall off the social ladder, I jumped. You see, I don't really exist. I'm off the grid: I have no documents - no bank statements, no utility bills, no driver's licence, passport, social security number - all that rubbish. For all the state knows about me, I might as well be a figment of your imagination,' he made a strange attempt at an amused expression. 'I can recommend this life. You should try it sometime.'

'I'm afraid that I'm not quite ready not to exist.'

He laughed, a broad and generous guffaw that progressed into a tubercular wheezing.

You may think me credulous, but, in the end, I believed him. He was a cubist painting of a man; you couldn't pin him down or define him from a single point of view - he was many men. I saw him mainly as a libertarian anarchist, a *Walden Pond* individualist, who resisted the supremacy of the state. Yet, during his time as a bank manager - according to his account - he had acted as a Robin Hood kind of socialist, redistributing wealth from the rich to the poor. The more that I talked to him, I began to detect some surprisingly unusual opinions. For instance, he had no time for soft drugs, such as marijuana or even alcohol. 'My body is my temple,' he would say. He wouldn't take any vaccines and didn't value medical science. 'Life is to be lived, not sustained artificially,' he told me. Yet, despite this, he lived off unhygienic scraps left in rubbish bins, discarded by the relatively prosperous.

I must admit that I began to be dismayed whenever Duffield wasn't there, on the park bench, sitting, waiting for me. I had started to look forward to meeting him, despite his unsavoury habits and wayward opinions. His lifestyle was so precarious. 'It's the bride price of my freedom,' he remarked. He had a taste for the cryptic.

Goodness knows how he had found out that I was a writer, but he had. It seemed to amuse him.

'Now, if you put me into a story, Charles, be sure to call me Duffield. Just that, nothing else. After all, if I am to represent your rather atrophied conscience, you have to use my real name.' His mouth twitched spasmodically somewhere in the depth of his beard.

'You flatter yourself if you imagine that I am going to include you in one of my stories.' I was a little gratified to see the evident disappointment on his face.

I was thinking of Duffield a few days later, when I went into my local Oxfam shop. I had intended to buy him a warm coat to replace his tattered gaberdine, but, instead, I gravitated towards the book section. When I saw one of my own titles, I felt a brief moment of pride. It was in mint condition, as if it hadn't been read. I opened the front cover. The price, written in faint pencil on the fly sheet, was 5p. The discovery that my books were of so little value depressed me. I shamefacedly bought my own book to prevent other people from discovering my Oxfam market value. I hid it in the attic, away from prying eyes. The embarrassment gradually faded into a general moroseness. I started to question and doubt my achievements. What did it matter if I was a published author? Who cared? At the age of seventy-two, I had to admit that I was most probably on my penultimate lap. I could no longer depend on income from my royalties - they had dwindled to a trickle. If it wasn't for my pension, I wouldn't be able to manage.

I brooded over this for several days, growing more and more depressed. I wanted to know what Duffield thought - surely, a man like him, who had jettisoned achievement for the sake of some bizarre notion about freedom, would have some interesting perspectives on unrealised ambition.

The day that I next met him was fresh, full of the heady scent of spring. Birds were calling each other in a frenzy of sexual energy, and it felt as if all of nature was writhing with fecundity, every bud bursting into leaf. The infinite blue of the sky was punctured with a tumble of cumulous clouds, drifting by with majestic slowness, and layers of wispy cirrus, barely moving, lay at a great height above them, with unbounded space beyond. Yet I was downcast.

'Oh...' Duffield laughed, 'the millennium blues. You've got it bad...' I shambled up to the park bench and sat down, dejected, beside him. 'What's bothering you this time?'

I resented his power over me. It was intolerable. Yet, in my vulnerable condition, his words brushed gently against me, filtered all my sorrows, shepherding my doubts towards a sense of revelation that I reluctantly embraced. I was sorry for myself.

'I feel that I have failed. In everything.'

Duffield looked at me tenderly, even with a certain amount of pity. 'I suspect that you, like me, have never achieved the one thing that we are all born able to do. It's the simplest of things. You see, there's a difference between giving someone a moment's pleasure and making them truly happy over time.' He paused, then added, perhaps a little too acidly, 'Maybe you've never made another person, except perhaps your parents, really happy.'

The remark pierced me. It was true: my ex-wife despised me; my son, Jonah, didn't want to know me; the only family member that I saw regularly was Emily, my wonderfully stubborn and forbearing daughter. 'That's a pretty damning indictment,' I said, my body feeling limp and defeated.

'Look at me, Charles. Look at my lifestyle. For God's sake, I'm not all that different from you.' Somehow, that wasn't as reassuring as it was intended to be.

I resolved to make more of an effort to show Emily how much I appreciated her. The opportunity arose a few days later, when she called round with a bunch of daffodils that she had picked from her garden. She breezed into my apartment as if she owned it. She started tidying up my notes for a story, that lay scattered around my table. I suppressed my urge to protest.

'I thought that even *you* would enjoy this golden host,'

she said, filling a vase of water for the blossoms.

I gave her a beatific smile. 'They do look wonderful.'

She gave me a sideways glance. 'Hmph.'

'And you do as well, darling.'

'What?'

'Look wonderful. You always do.' I arranged my face into what I imagined was a radiant smile that expressed my love for her.

'Dad, are you ill? You are being completely weird today. Has something happened?'

'No. Nothing out of the ordinary. I just wanted to show you that... I... *appreciate* you.' Another smile. Goodness knows why I found it so difficult to say, 'that I love you'.

'Well, that's...' her attention was too entirely focussed on arranging the daffodils to complete the sentence. 'There! That's better. They should be good for a week. Sorry, Dad. You were saying...?'

I felt deflated. 'It doesn't matter.'

I reported this exchange to Duffield, who chortled so much that he almost choked, a vast quantity of spittle clinging to his beard.

'That's priceless,' he spluttered.

'I don't know why you are so bloody amused.'

'Don't you understand?' he gave me that unsteady glance, like a flickering torch. 'You can't just impose your love. You have to be true to yourself at the same time.'

'That could be difficult.'

'The simplest things normally are.'

Duffield's words made a deep impression on me, and I dwelt on them for several days. I resolved to buy Emily a present, something that would mean a lot to her personally, rather than something that would simply make a hole in my pocket. I remembered how, when she was a child, I used to read her bedtime stories. Her favourite was Dickens. She had loved *Great Expectations, A Tale of Two Cities, Oliver Twist* - I read them to her over and over again, waiting until her petite eyelids would droop as she drifted off to sleep to the sound of my voice.

My thoughts turned to the relationships that daughters had with their flawed fathers: *King Lear*? Mr Woodhouse in *Emma*? Neither of these seemed to fit. Then it came to me: I would buy her a copy of Dickens's *Little Dorrit*. A dutiful daughter with an impossibly self-centred father - she would understand. I eventually discovered a beautiful, leather-bound first edition in an antiquarian bookshop on Charing Cross Road. They wrapped it in scented tissue, as if it was a religious relic.

As I later told Duffield, when I recounted the story of how Emily responded, her initial reaction when she saw the volume was one of delight.

'It's one of my absolutely favourite novels,' she said. 'How did you know?' Then she noticed that it was a first edition. 'My goodness, this must have cost a fortune. Dad, you aren't seriously ill, are you? Please tell me that you aren't! I don't know how I would feel if I lost you.'

'No, darling, you don't have to worry about that. As far as I know, I am perfectly shipshape in the health department.'

Her body relaxed, and she made a small 'phew' sound as she expelled some pent-up air. Then she began to examine the book.

'It's absolutely charming. I can't tell you how much this means to me...' She paused. A look of suspicion flitted across her face. 'You aren't up to anything, are you? Some trick or other...'

'Emily,' I was surprised by the sudden tightening of my throat as I spoke her name, 'I just wanted to show you how much you mean to me, that's all.'

She approached me silently, without speaking, and put

her arms around my neck. 'You are a silly billy sometimes, Dad. Of course, I know that you love me, stubborn old goat that you are. You don't need to prove it to me like this. But...' and it was her turn to get emotional, 'I will cherish this gift as long as I live. Absolutely,' and she planted a kiss on my forehead. 'There now,' she shook her head vigorously, 'enough of this sentimental nonsense. I bet that you haven't changed the water in those daffodils all week!'

Duffield had listened attentively. I waited for words of approval; none came. Eventually he said, 'That Emily of yours is quite a treasure, isn't she?'

I had shown Duffield sides of myself that I had never revealed to anyone else. In the process, we had become close. But I always looked at him as separate from me, a curiosity rather than a genuine friend. I had made an effort with Emily, now I needed to make an effort with Duffield.

I walked into the bathroom and stared into the mirror. I had used this method many times to get closer to a character. There was a trick to it. I relaxed the muscles of my eyes, defocussing and staring straight ahead. Slowly the edges of my vision darkened, as if I was looking down a dark tunnel. Whiskers sprouted from my face and my skin began to look weathered by the sun and rain. The bathroom mirror faded from view. I *was* Duffield, I *became* him. Perhaps, in a way, I always had been. I even spoke with his voice.

'Hello, Charles,' I said.

I imagined Dewington sitting on that park bench, waiting for me where we usually met. He had printed out the story, the one called, simply, 'Duffield'. He handed me the pages, 'I wanted you to be the first to read it. It's about our unlikely friendship. It's something remarkable, you know.' He was excited, a little breathless, as if he had just been running, rather than sitting, waiting.

His words moved me. I had never expected him to acknowledge that we had become real friends. People generally avoid the homeless - we have a deadly disease that they might catch.

'I lied when I said that you wouldn't feature in a story,' Dewington carried on. 'I'm sorry. I thought I could use you, plunder your thoughts, build a character out of little bits of you blended with little bits of me. The one thing that I learnt from you is that friendship is something mutual, but, instead, I exploited you. Forgive me. I hope that this,' he gestured towards the papers in my hands, 'makes up for things.'

I glanced at the first line.

Duffield once told me that he had been a bank manager.

I was happy. I felt the pleasure surging through me, like the sap rising in a tree. If you are living on the streets, you don't exist, nobody sees you. Then someone, somewhere notices you: it makes all the difference. My mouth gave a spasmodic twitch buried amongst my whiskers.

Printed in Great Britain
by Amazon